MW01126599

A Violin's Secret

by

Dr. Scott Young

Copyright © 2018 Dr. Scott Young

A Violin's Secret

All rights reserved.

No part of this publication (book) may be reproduced, stored in a retrieval system, or be transmitted in any form, or by any means, electronic, mechanical, photocopying or otherwise without the prior written consent of the author, Dr. Scott Young, or the publisher, Logos to Rhema Publishing.

Written permission must be secured from the publisher or author to use or reproduce any part of this book, except for the inclusion of brief quotations in critical reviews or articles.

Scripture quotations noted in King James Version of the Bible.

ISBN: 9781724145864

Published in the United States of America by:
Susan Reidel, Logos to Rhema
Sreidel@hotmail.com

ACKNOWLEDGEMENTS

To my wonderful son who has thought about this story and suggested the book cover.   Thank you to my mother who spurred me toward a lifelong desire to study World War II. I also want to thank my wife for reading my stories and being honest with all criticism to make the story better. I called the beautiful retirement center, Concordia on the Lake in Lakewood Colorado and asked permission to use their name for my character to live. They had read the story and they gave me their blessing. My main fictional character would live there and walk about its lake. I saw it in a vision that I still cannot explain.

Dr. Scott Young, CCC-A, FAAA
www.heartulsa.com
www.drscottyoung.com

Dr. Scott Young

PREFACE

After my vocation as an Audiologist (one who treats hearing loss with hearing aid technology), I have studied three major areas: music, eschatology (study of Biblical end times) and World War II. All of my life my mother and I would read or watch anything to do with World War II. Her father would not let her know anything about the war while it was happening when she was a small child (mostly related to silly reasoning). She spent much of her adult years studying it which encouraged in me that same research habit.

In 1991, I glanced at a TV documentary which showed Auschwitz's rows of the buildings during World War II. This short image, of which some original buildings are still erect, hit me in the gut. I ran to a pad beside my computer but kept an eye on the TV screen and jotted a few notes which led to a short story, about which was expanded into this story. In the later 1990's, my father received an award in Washington DC, and he invited the whole family to witness it. At the first touristy chance of the trip, I dragged the family to the Holocaust Museum. I stopped at an amazing display in the front of a punch card machine that I later learned that IBM helped the Nazis (*IBM and the Holocaust* by Michael Hirsh) to propagate the effective transfer of human beings by cattle cars to their deaths. These punch cards were the first uses of calculators and computing in mass effectiveness (if you will pardon this usage of effectiveness relating to the killing of six million Jews and five million other undesirables, mentally ill, political dissidents, and gypsies throughout northern Europe).

This museum gave a disturbing message when you moved through it from the top level to the bottom; that the Christians had pushed forward the killing of the Jews. There were and still are sick groups of people including the Spanish Inquisition, Nazis and even the Pope of World War II who were either actively killing Jews or turning a blind eye to it throughout the centuries.

I also took the opportunity to stand within an actual cattle car. The museum allowed visitors to walk around it, but I partially blocked passage of individuals in the middle of the car. I closed my eyes and smelled the wood, felt the surfaces, and listened for the creaks it made trying to capture all the senses available in this forsaken car originally meant for animals.

Anyone who studies the Holocaust will also note that there were Catholic priests, pastors, musicians, carpenters and homemakers who risked their lives to hide the Jews, because they realized that saving God's people was a spiritual mandate; they paid for this decision with their lives. Satan always has had it in for the Jewish people from the beginning of time to now. The Holocaust is the most current manifestation of that hatred. Of course, all are God's creatures so we should always protect the innocent and weak. The Jews were and always have been a special case. What I wanted to highlight is one fictional family's representation of a choice between protecting themselves and protecting the innocent. Too many times people of the Baby Boomer as well as the X and Y generations have not experienced the horrors the Greatest Generation (as Tom Brokaw coined) has felt as a result of World War II. I wanted the later generations to see this timeframe one more time while not losing one's faith in the loss of circumstance.

The question every reader must ask and be forced to answer is this: can a God who loves this world and gave his Son exist, when evil circumstances try to separate us from the greater reality of a spiritual certainty that can undergird us?

CHAPTER 1

Ernst took the familiar stroll around Concordia on the Lake – a wonderful retirement center -- in south Denver, Colorado. Even though the Rockies were nearing winter, he lost most of the feeling for the cold long ago. His extremities never really got used to it, but heart surgery years ago gave him the feeling of imperviousness to cold. Denver was always beautiful in white, although the cold of this winter began to bite. The Channel Nine announced that Denver would have a biting winter that felt similar to the way he felt. His life was beginning to grow as frigid as was his liver.

His brisk walks around the Lake near the Concordia were perfect for his mind, but probably not his body. Physicians told him that he needed to take it easy and not exercise as much. But slowing was not an option in his youth and it wouldn't be today either, no matter that he had liver cancer.

It was funny since Ernst liked to know much about bodily functions during his years of studying anything that might come to mind, but the liver's function had escaped him until Dr. Willingham explained its function. He found that the liver sent the waste out which humored Ernst, because his youth smashed his future. In his youth, harmful substances were plentiful daily; in this day and age, he hardly ate the horrid hamburgers fried in most restaurants. His grandchild, Axel, many times could find nothing to eat on a menu without the bastardized sandwich, but Ernst always found lettuce with a touch of ranch to whet his appetite correctly. If he had died of liver cancer as a teenager, it would have been fitting.

The *walk* could be physically exhausting but always mentally uplifting. The liver cancer plagued his thoughts to distraction. On this day, in the beginning of October, marked a course correction: he would have to tell Dr. Willingham to lay off. His daughter, Rachel, pushed Ernst to see another Physician for a second opinion. He knew the first doc was correct in his diagnosis, but it hardened his resolve to turn out the lights on his life. Not that it bothered him to die, but his blood carried more death than life.

"Don't you remember, Ileana, when a piece of bread in the dirt was life? I know you did darling..." he mused to his long deceased wife as if she were strutting beside moving her scarf around her neck tighter breaking the cold walk's grip around the lake.

Ernst had few to call on him like some of the women in Lake View. Some received visits from many relatives. Ernst had sometimes regretted the fact that he had so few kin to his name but cherished the few he did have. When Rachel brought Axel, he would push off into his strolls around the park where Axel would gleefully lead the way.

Axel would constantly whistle *Star Wars* (poorly Ernst silently added) as he ambled around the lake. While Ernst hadn't seen that silly show until 1998 when his grandson brought it by for the both of them to watch, he realized that the music took him back farther than he could have even imaged. Rachel had shown him on the *internet machine* from her phone that many of the *Star Wars* songs were written by John Williams patterned his compositions after Richard Wagner's technique to create a simple theme chording and building it up. He had felt for years, after he had seen *Star Wars* the first time with "Ride of the Valkyries" by Wagner that John Williams had borrowed more than the technique, not to mention many of the same musical structures. Axel began to toot the damnable theme *Star Wars*, Ernst would think of Wagner, then the concentration camps.

When he even tried to explain this to those of his generation who lived through the War, almost no one would understand because few had lived it. Some of his friends in Concordia had seen camps, because they had helped to liberate them, but very few lived *in* them. Ernst had survived them for almost two years. Hence, the reason why liver cancer was little more than a passing thought to him since he should have died years ago; but God had given him a reprieve.

The walk gave him clarity: to remember and sometimes to forget. When he read his Bible, *Romans* mentioned that we should not concentrate on "vain imaginations."

"That's right Ileana," Ernst mused over his left shoulder. "I know that considering the *what might-have-beens* or the *could-have-beens* are useless. I know that I should be more tolerant for them, but I can't feel that way now that the decision has been made. I'm coming home soon." At once he closed his eyes and stopping his pace to pray that God would have a spirit of forgetfulness until he realized that His name was Grace who would remember nothing of his sin.

More as the *end* of his life crept into specific existence (not a known date he would quip but a more definite end such as dying very old in one's own bed), Ernst used his walk for reflection of his life in the camp. Those *Star Wars* songs would remind him as well as the irony of dying now of liver cancer instead of back then. The more that he walked the Lake, the more he talked more to his wife, because she would want to spruce up his side of the mansion when he got there. Other times, it was Mother and Father, and sometimes it was his elementary teacher back in Ulm, Germany near the Danube River.

He was not crazy (he would remind himself) but had read that 50% of the population routinely talked out loud to themselves. He just added a silent personality. Interestingly, when someone like Rachel or Axel came along, he talked very little. With the certainty of his condition and his desire against medical treatment, Axel needed to hear the *Story*. Rachel wanted to hear the *Story,* but he wasn't sure that he would tell her. He had no idea why he had not told her but that he had felt that he was correct in not doing so.

"Ileana, don't pester me, because I have have good reasons why I am doing what I am doing. I shouldn't have to explain it to you!" suddenly chiding her perceived pang of guilt placed upon his shoulders.

So Ernst prepared himself by rehearsing the *Story* to Axel to get it correct. He could even ask the questions of those invisible relatives to fill in the gaps he felt were important. Many times after bringing the query aloud to his Father, he would hear the answer a few seconds later.

He walked back to Concordia on a late morning to start the important day. The beginning of walking around the lake wasn't really considered the start of the day, because his thoughts in the morning were always jumbled. Ernst felt that his day began when he walked back into Concordia. He passed by the postman who was beginning to make his mail deliveries. Mail time was a big event in Concordia since that was most of the residents' only chance for contact with the outside world.

In Concordia, few used that "wholly impersonal contraption" email (as Ernst thought of it). Therefore, the mailman could feel the mob of eyes lusting after the possibility of his treasures, much as was known in barracks around the world through every war-weary soldier seeking that letter from the sweetheart. Ernst believed that regular mail was a ritual of an older era dying off.

Ernst would have liked most of the mailmen, but Todd bothered him. Ernst couldn't imagine the reason for desecrating one's body with tattoos of *metal bands* that wouldn't even be remembered in the future.

"Haven't I shown you *my* tattoo, Todd? Didn't you see what they did to me? How could you allow it to be done to you?" Ernst shivered at the thought of Todd entering the building as his walking partner changed faces again.   Todd tended to patronizingly ignore any rebuffs of Ernst and went about his business as dutifully as possible. Only when Todd came into view did he snap into the present.

"No mail for you today, sir," Todd pushed by the front feeding frenzy of packages not for Ernst.

Ernst then passed by the crowd around Todd's approach to get to the elevator to his apartment on the third floor.   He showered and shaved, stopping to smell aftershave that he purchased but never used which was somewhat like the one his father used before the war.   Ernst regarded his visage in the mirror as he smelled the aftershave: he was five foot, ten inches with a wispy-looking constitution around 155 pounds. His eyebrows were now bushy and the top of his skull showed his thinning hair.   Ernst never felt that he was much to look at, but the girls here loved his skill with a violin. He had played all his life and even would update his playing style with the times.

Unlike some musicians who couldn't change to any style, Ernst could play the violin with many types of music and enjoyed it from time to time. His passion in music was close to his inner voice in which he kept his repartee with his God. The Bible talked about "praying without ceasing" and he endeavored to do so; he could also "play without ceasing". His prayer life and his violin were the only things that kept him alive in the camps, spiritually as well as physically. Some came from the camps spiritually bankrupt.

Some lived in this day and age soulfully foreclosed more out of choice with so many distractions dueling for one's attention: Netflix, computers or cell phones. But many who came out of the camps more than 70 years ago had lost their will and their God. He thanked God that he was younger and didn't have to watch his children or grandchildren see death like he had seen. He put the bow against the strings.

A Violin's Secret

CHAPTER 2

Playing the violin pushed his memories of the camps to the forefront with even greater focus. Even if he didn't know which song to play, a variety of melodies and runs up the bridge would start it out as it was before his recitation. The violin always brought clarity. Ernst prayed, "God let me know the words I need to tell Axel. I have little money left over to give him, but I do have history to share. Let me share it; give me the courage to share it this once."

Almost without knowing he had done so, he put away his violin and picked up the phone to dial his daughter and set a morning date with his grandson to tell him the *Story,* and only him.

"Sure, dad, anytime you want to talk to him; he loves talking to you. You know I loved to listen to you tell about your younger years. I don't understand why I can't listen in and why you are giving up on life..." Rachel trailed off.

"I know, I know. I feel that it is my time."

"Your time for what? To die? Dad, would you please go to the doctor to see what kinds of surgeries they could do?" Rachel begged.

"I have already told you of my decision to not receive resuscitation or any surgical procedures. I have prayed about it longer than you know, and I know it is near my time," Ernst claimed.

"I love you dad...and Axel does too. Larry and I want you to see him graduate, to see him marry...unlike mom, I don't want to push you since that never worked for her," tears began to muddle the conversation.

"I love you as well, honey. I will see you on Thursday then?"

"OK..." he had hung up the phone before she had more to try to convince him of.

Ernst then walked to the kitchen table to sketch out his 9" by 11" monologue. Normally, one would ramble his own history with stops and starts. For Axel's sake, he would outline in detail the path his life wove to create continuity.

"Darling, remind me of the *Story* so that I can tell them both. You know I wanted only to tell Axel, but I see that you desire me to tell our daughter as well," speaking as if Ileana was behind him then he almost sensed her voice over his shoulder or maybe it was from the Lord.

"*I was born to loving parents in Ulm, Germany. Remember to tell them of the school teacher and the Violin; the replacement teacher; the betrayal and the camps; and then the long march to nowhere,*" spoken to his heart as if he were saying it. Since that first nightmare diagnosis of cancer it was as if the long lost characters were chirping more usual now. He jotted down those points on a scratch pad, and put it in his right pant pocket.

Sometimes, musicians might begin to play their instruments without much conscious thought as Ernst did. At first the more familiar melodies or a series of chord structures which are taken from many pieces, then on to more stringent pieces. This activity cleared his mind from the interference of the world and brought a focused light upon only the music. Then Ernst began the tune that he wrote in the woods outside of Ulm, more than 70 years ago. While it wasn't even that good a ditty, it wafted, as the smell of a scented candle could, to seize the intellect of a 13-year-old boy in love with woman who didn't even know it. He might have played it, no more than two minutes long, three times through without even knowing it when he realized that his subconscious released its hold: it was 3:30 and almost time for his diagnosis on the second opinion. He realized that might take him almost 20 minutes to travel five miles in Denver traffic that approached the rush hour.

He put his violin away and grabbed his car keys that were within his jacket. At the clinic, there was always a wait. No matter how he timed it, Ernst felt the pang of waiting. It reminded him, just a little, of interring in the camp. In Dachau, one waited for the morning roster to be called, for the evening roster calling, for monthly medical inspections, and for many other activities. Many of those activities could lead to one's death at any point in time, so one could suppose he had *post-traumatic stress* associated with doctor's offices. He knew of friends who had fought for the Americans in WWII who had their own stresses, such as hitting the deck when an automobile backfired. New cars didn't do that anymore, but back after the war, many automobiles would almost routinely do so. It drove many of his friend's eyes shut to resist the urge to *duck and cover* with those types of noises.

"I guess that's why I hate these places," Ernst quietly announced almost under his breath.

"I hate 'em too," a teen of around 14 said beside him.

"Why are they talking to you today?" Ernst leaned in conspiratorially.

"They talk to my dad many times but have to tell me their version as well. They want to tell me that Dad is going to be fine, 'ya know? Like I really believe them!" the boy flipped back a black lock of hair shocked into the background of a blonde head.

"Maybe they are telling the truth," Ernst said with poor conviction in his tone.

"He has been here before, and they said he was going to be fine. I am sick of the *yo-yo* with him being sick again and then not. We're always worrying that the *sick* will be back soon," the teen turned away allowing the black lock to cover a tear, as Ernst placed a knowing hand upon the youth's right shoulder.

Ernst name was finally called, even though they called him "Ernie" because so few in America could pronounce his name without more than the cursory glance. When he was led back to *Exam Room 3,* he resolved not to go forward with anymore treatment as he had chosen no matter what they said. But this was the time to steel the plan.

He felt that God had brought that boy in his life for a reason, as he ambled back to the room behind the nurse. He rarely ignored small signs, and he felt strongly that God was speaking through that boy's pain. He would not inflict that on Rachel and Axel.

"Well, you are in the middle stages of liver disease; I do believe that an effective round of chemo and possibly surgery after chemo might be an excellent treatment plan. I will tell my nurse to schedule you for your first chemo. She will also give you all that you need to know about..." Dr. Willingham was cut off in mid-sentence.

"I am not going through with any treatment; my time is shortly coming," Ernst stated matter-of-factly.

"There are many fears I am sure that you have that my nurse, Debbie, will put to rest..."

"I am not fearful of death; it has followed me for years. It is time though, I know that now."

"I hear that from many of my patients like yourself but..."

"I am sure you do and now you are going to tell me that I can live many months or a few years with treatment. What you don't realize is that I am not going to argue with you, but I have decided. Thanks for your time," Ernst stood up and left *Exam Room 3* for good in his mind with a stupefied Physician in his wake. Ernst was sure that Dr. Willingham hadn't been talked to in that way by any patient.

Ernst was the last man to be rude to people; but since his 20's, he really didn't take orders from most in authority. It was not that he would break the law, but most rules were the last things that he followed, except for his own. That is why his own furniture store against the purple mountains had been his haven. He owned it for forty-five years. It was never big like those huge chains, but his customers loved him just the same for the quality and craftsmanship, even the repairs that he would do when no one else would take repairs anymore. Ernst would complete them until the chains moved in next door and dwindled his client base. He closed his store only eight years ago, after Ileana died, and retired after the chain bought out the space that he had owned for their own growth. The only good that came out of it was that he was able to retire, with at least some money to get by on.

He was in the elevator as the lady from the front desk called for him to talk to this Debbie. He pretended not to hear her since he didn't really want to be rude, but no one would talk him out of this course. It was a good course; it was a right course. He was through with his life soon and wanted to firm up things with Axel most of all.

CHAPTER 3

Ernst prepared for Thursday morning with a coat and gloves by the entry hall's chair. It was almost as if he were laying his clothes out for his funeral, except that the dead was giving the eulogy.

Axel bounded through the door that was left cracked open, as was Ernst's tradition when he expected his family. He barreled into Ernst angling higher than his height for a *lift-up hug*.

"Honey, don't do that to papa, you might hurt his back!" Rachel called to Axel without avail.

"It's aallll riight," as Ernst strained to pick him up near the couch arm to support his back.

"Papa!"

"Papa loves you, do you know that?"

"Yeah!"

"What did the doc say," Rachel seamlessly asked while trying to put a dish in the dishwasher to make the question nonchalant.

"Ah, I don't need their opinions, I have my own," smiling into Axel's face.

"Dad...what did you say to them?" accused Rachel.

"I said no."

"Why, dad?"

"I don't want to talk about that now, later there will be time for the trivial," Ernst trailed off.

16

"You call your health trivial as well as walking out on your doctor?"

"Did you check up on me again? It doesn't matter though."

"Whaddaya talking about, papa? Are the doctors going to fix you up? Mom says that you need them to fix you; says that you liver doesn't work. Are you going to be around for a long time?" Axel was seven years old and bright; he could also try your patience with the bubbling questions without respite.

The boy couldn't imagine a life without his parents and Papa. His Papa was the one person who he could open up to and tell him all that was rattling around in his skull. No one had more good things to say to situations than his Papa.

"I'll be here for a while longer yet, but you and I have some important things to talk about...about my past," brightness in Ernst's eyes lit up like Rachel hadn't seen when discussing anything such as his past.

Rachel knew where this was going, him setting up some type of last will and testament speech, so she put her discussion of Physicians aside to focus on his intensity regarding the past. She had heard a precious few stories. All Rachel knew was that her dad had grown up in Ulm, Germany, and that he was a young teenager during World War II. She also knew that he spent time in Dachau concentration camp for two years.

He would not talk of his experiences, so Rachel studied everything she could get her hands on about World War II. She took local classes at Auraria Community College which would have several themes on concentration camps and overall strategies of World War II. She also watched every show on the History Channel on any war topic. She wondered if it was just a sick fascination regarding what happened. She knew that all the knowledge she gained brought her one step closer to knowing her father who was more silent than a bad satellite signal in a storm.

Her husband, Larry, was an Audiologist working for a private practice in Denver who had fitted Ernst with his first pair of Completely-In-the-Canal (CIC) hearing aids that he wore faithfully. Larry would also sit and watch the shows about World War II, but not with the studiousness that Rachel applied to it. Larry would relay stories of men who were his patients getting hearing aids.

One man that Larry talked to told him that two weeks after the Normandy landings in France. This man led three German soldier toward the rear for interrogation, but he found out that during the march he only had one round left in his rifle. He shook as he trudged with his charges back two miles but never let it show to the prisoners in front of him. Larry said that this man never even told his kids or his wife that story. The man said that he didn't even know why he told Larry except that he was a good man and he loved the digital hearing aids he had from Larry. Larry tried to remember to relay any story of World War II to Rachel, much to Rachel's delight since her father would not give her any of the detail these patients would give. Sometimes Rachel would sulk after hearing these amazing stories of the *Greatest Generation* always wishing that her father would tell his daughter one of the most important parts of his life.

"Let's begin our walk, Axel," Ernst said.

"Dad...could I...I would really like to go with you two," Rachel pleaded in a tearful whisper with drops leaking from her eyes.

"I would be honored to have you...both of you along. Your mother would want you to know as well!" Ernst proclaimed.

Axel beamed since it was one of those rare times in a child's life that *he* would be included in on an important meeting. Normally, it was the grownups who had these types of talk time, not Axel. Rachel, quietly satisfied and choking back those tears of happiness that might break out into golf claps, helped Ernst with his coat first as Axel threw his coat on as if the first major blizzard of the winter was here and he had snowballs to make. Axel almost ran ahead too fast out of the apartment but remembered quickly enough to hold the door for his papa and mother as they walked into the blue skies of a Colorado late fall day. Many never realize that most days in Colorado in the fall and winter aren't really that cold since the sky is so clear with low humidity. Even a day at 34 degrees Fahrenheit could be a beautifully clear morning that was comfortable when wearing a coat.

Ernst headed with purpose toward the lake's mile and a half route broken up by several docks allowing for bird watching. He hurriedly reached into his pocket to feel for the notes that he had taken to remind him of his meeting. When he found it crinkle against his hand's search, he relaxed.

"I will tell you about my life. I know that I have had so few discussions of this type, but if you had lived my life, you would speak little of it as well. I don't have a lot of money to give you, but a history is what I wish to pass to you as well as my violin," Ernst began.

"Your violin!" Axel beamed while throwing his hands to his face in a gasp of joy.

"Yes, my violin. My violin will mean nothing to you if you don't know its history. They say that a car is an antique when it goes beyond twenty years; I think instruments need more like forty. But to have and cherish a violin such as mine, one must understand its history. You might go to a music store and see many new instruments, but the ones that have real beauty are the ones whose history have survived with it. The wood even remembers the tears and the laughs, as well as the good melodies played upon it.

"If you play too many bad songs upon it, you will stain its ability to hear good music. I know that you don't really understand since you are just beginning to play your own violin. Your mom has told me that last year you have started with your teacher Ms. Bobbie Nelson. Mom says that you are really starting to get the hang of it. Is that right?"

"Yes, Papa. I can't play like you do, but I can play 'Twinkle, Twinkle, Little Star'. You wanna hear it when we get back to your house?"

"Yes, I would," Ernst wrapped his arms around Axel's shoulders. Ernst glanced at Rachel who walked with a contemplative look as if soaking all in for a crucial final exam. He pressed on, circling back into his introduction.

"To play an instrument is only the beginning. You must breathe with it…"

"Why do I have to breathe on my violin?" Axel scrunched his face with confusion.

"No, *breathe with it* means to make it a part of you. You are not really playing the notes, but your fingers are communicating with your strings directly without having to think about it. You won't understand now, but you will in the future," he decided not to explain it further since Rachel was nodding her head in understanding. Ernst finally realized that bringing Rachel was the right choice; her mother always had led him down the correct path. "Axel, have you noticed the deep scratches on my violin?"

"You mean the one that goes up and down on the front of it?"

"That's just one of them!"

"Dad, why haven't you ever repaired it?" Rachel asked.

"Sometimes women have plastic surgery to correct the shape of their nose or varicose veins to make themselves more beautiful. Your car might need a body shop to pull out the dents incurred from bumping it into the side of your garage…" Ernst broke off with a wink and a twinkle in the other eye, because Rachel had done that very thing to her new Honda Accord last month. Rachel blushed, then slapped her dad's left shoulder.

"But, violins don't need repairs like that. Most scratches never affect the tune or the timbre of an instrument. What's more, it is its own badge of courage: its tattoo. You have seen my tattoo on my arm haven't you, Axel?" Ernst tapped his right forearm with the numbered tattoo *113589*.

"Is that number your locker combo, Papa?" Axel seriously asked.

Both Rachel and Ernst laughed at the extremely well meant question Axel posed based upon his experience.

"No, little buddy. It was tattooed on my arm by the Nazi's back in the war."

"Why'd they do that?"

"They wanted to show who I was. During that time I was called...when I was called out by the guards as *113589*. They didn't like my name as much as the number..." Ernst trailed off with more pain in his voice than he realized after so much time.

"But..." Axel was stopped from asking his next series of questions by his mother's hand upon his shoulders and a shaking of her head.

"The tattoo was a reminder just like the scratches are for my violin, of what we went through all those years ago in the war. You see some people can't love others as God intended. Some well-meaning people have wanted to remove my scars, but I refused. It makes me who I am. I know it is hard for you to understand this."

"You mean the way my belly button doesn't stay in good 'cause I don't have to keep lint," Axel stated.

"That is somewhat like it. You would not be you without your belly button out," Ernst playfully poked Axel's belly button with a short giggle.

"Why do we need to remember bad things, Papa?"

"Most bad things we probably don't *want* to remember. Some things are so important that we must keep them to remember for the next generation, like you. Jesus had scars on his hands and feet after He was resurrected, so that we would always remember that His death was the price for our sin. Now, while my tattoo isn't *as* meaningful as Jesus', it still reminds me to never forget those who died in the camps," a tear formed in Ernst's left eye and began to fall.

When Rachel saw the tear, she felt a welling up in both of her eyes as the empathy for her father's past was being poured out for her ears. She could have been irritated that he never would share this type of intimacy when she was a child, but her eyes and heart swam in this moment.

"I want to tell you how my violin saved my mind; how my God brought me through my younger years, somewhat older than you are right now; and how your great-grandparents live..."

CHAPTER 4

1942 in Ulm, Germany

I knew that two things were going to occupy me for hours upon end: my violin coming on my birthday and my teacher. Both were beautiful to me; both stole my heart and made my forearms tingle.

It was early fall near the Danube River, which most people in my town just called *The River.* I am within ten days of being twelve years old that no child ever forgets. It is the most glorious time of the year with all the trees dancing from the river wind with yellow and red leaves praising within their movements.

This year a new teacher will come to my class. There hasn't been a teaching change for years, but father says the world's craziness brings about a wandering spirit in most people. He says that some people will move from the city to the smaller towns for peace.

I thought I knew what peace was *before,* but all of that had changed: scrunched up faces scurrying about with less purpose and more of a faster pace to their walk. I would only walk at a fast pace to finish my chores to run to the woods nearby our house.

Sitting and listening to the trees could calm the fast pace out of me in a hurry. I started my love for music by listening to the woods. The winter trees would crack like a marching parade; the summer and spring leaves would clap for a conquering hero in a rhythmic fashion. The fall had a rhythm all its own. The leaves were more brittle and the rustle made them swirl off the trees which added another sound to those who listened. My sister, Katrina, would pull her curls out while listening but never seemed to hear God's music. I was wiser than her ears were. After a short time (never short enough for me with her incessant chattering), she would leave for the house. I was left to hear the next verse the trees would sing. Actually, it was more like a musical with the dancing and the songs I heard.

I had been taking lessons with an older violin from my father who was the church's music leader. They could only afford a head pastor. My father, Frederick, was a great musician and a song leader. Sometimes, I had the opportunity to play along on the violin to his piano at services. He played with more passion in one service than I thought I could ever know. I realized years later that the passion that he played with was as a model for me to follow. I wasn't sure if he knew it then, but his passion was an available energy to tap into.

Then my father began to explode my world. He informed me that the "older violin" I had been playing was really not that old (although it looked old and ragged from overuse). My father was going to make it new again. He was a wonderful craftsman as well, but I never could develop his touch for woodworking. I obliged him in dutifully grabbing each tool when needed, even if it was the wrong one. Although it was our town's proud custom to take your father's trade, my father knew that I had an affinity for music and not woodworking; he never pushed his craft upon me.

I blathered to all my friends that I was receiving the best violin in Germany for my birthday until my voice wearied them. My friends begged me to stop the details of the repair while walking toward the soccer. The constant succor of music that I could hear in my head increased within the woods between Werner's and my house.

When my birthday arrived, I bounded down the stairs three at a time until I woke everyone. I tried to even pull the eggs out to help mother cook breakfast trying to be helpful only to break two of them on the way to the sink. I was of no use to my mother in the kitchen, and she let me know it with only mock irritation knowing how much this day meant to me. I even straightened father's notes he scattered about his desk to give back in a small way what he was giving to me.

After breakfast which barely hit my tongue on the way down my throat, I waited for the rest of my family to finish theirs with much toe tapping. Katrina, being only four years old, twirled her food, much to my despair. My impatience forced Mother to scold her into eating.

"Well, here it is," my father beamed killing my despair of the wait while he handed me a blue cloth wrapping package.

With as much grace as I could muster, I gingerly peeled back the cloth to behold the most wonderful sight I had seen. An ornately carved violin. It was highly polished and gave a new timbre with new strings as well, as my index finger ran across the surface of the strings. My father tried to tell me of the history of the instrument and how he made it, but my ears were beyond listening and Mother knew it as she touched father's arm to silence.

"Play it, son," mother asked.

I played a conflagration of melodies melding into one slightly discordant tune, but I didn't care since they were the first sounds of my new violin. I hugged father with a loud, squealing and ungamely voice croaking *thank you.* Flinging the door open, I ran to introduce the woods to my violin. I knew the two would be the best of friends.

The next two weeks went by with no thought of friends and other than me hounding of Father to teach me more on my violin. I played night and day trying to perfect my skill, thinking that I might become a first seat player in the Ulm Orchestra and on to Berlin to take my place with the Greats. While I dreamed of orchestras to write and play, the world slowly began to darken for my parents each night at the dinner table.

They would talk of very little else, but the war and the brutalities in hushed tones, thinking that I couldn't hear when I had left the table. They discussed the sheltering of people that my father knew in the town since many were being sent to the camps. I thought that my father might be going mad since I knew that camps could be quite exhilarating, even believing that there might be one for a budding musician like me.

"Could I go to one of the camps you and mother talk about? Is there one for musicians?" I asked Father at supper.

My mother froze while still holding her hot skillet until she had to set it down quickly. Her face told me that she might backhand me. My father only looked with a rock solid expression of utter sternness while saying, "Those camps are not a place that anyone would desire to go."

"But father, Werner says that there is a camp ten miles from here,"

"Has he told you anything about the camp?" my father seriously asked.

"No. He says he knows no one knows who goes there, but we thought camp might be fun."

"These camps are not fun and you will stay away from there. Mind me, young man!"

"Yes, father," I responded and ate my potatoes in silence, not knowing what I said had violated the mood of my family for the night.

The next day Werner caught me later in the afternoon after our chores and had only one thing on his mind, "Let's take the forest route to the camp!"

"Father forbade me!" I pleaded against pressure-filled eyes.

"We won't tell him," sounded like a good enough reason to abandon my father's wisdom as well as to Werner's will.

We moved along the tree lines to find a trail we had all taken many a time. There were many more dried pinecones than I had remembered from years ago when I had walked this with my uncle and father hunting. They were so thick in many places that I barely saw the trail and

28

realized few were taking this path anymore. This fact made it all the more insatiable for boys to wind along it. We did so with a spy's fervor with one moving ahead in front of the other scouting the path with stealth our only companion.

When we reached a clearing through the wooded area, we saw a barbed wired fence. The assault on our nostrils made me gag; it was nearly indescribable. The odor was akin to pigs wallowing in their own excrement, mixed with all levels of despair one could conjure. There we stayed closer to the tree line behind the barbed wire fence so that the men in the guard towers would not see us.

"If this is the Wehrmacht, why would it smell this bad? My brother would never have been a part of this!" Werner exclaimed with pride and disgust at the same time in regarding his brother, who had just joined the army.

"Oh, this is horrible! Who could live here?" I held my nose as tightly as possible to no avail.

As if on cue, the gates were opened with the sounds of people pouring into them from an eastern direction which was beyond our sight. They looked so bedraggled that I couldn't see how any of them could have the energy to move as they did. The guard's rifle butts met many prisoners' backs forcing all within the doors a few hundred feet from our perch. We watched in stunned silence.

I backed away and broke one of those dry pinecones on the path we had traversed creating a loud crackle. The guards seemed spooked. Most people without weapons spooked around corners; guards with rifles, on the contrary, purposefully pointed their weapons in the crackle's direction. Both of us hit the ground and slinked back into the brush. The guards searched near our position for a long time, while we fearfully sweated through our cotton shirts before they called off their direction. As soon as they had left, it took us several minutes to get our legs to move again with our temporary bout of paralysis, but move we did back into the forest. This time we looked back pushing our footfalls faster than we could have believed. We still tried to make it back through the forests with stealth but more speed brought back the crackles under our feet.

"We can't tell my father what we did!" I spouted after we reached our property's clearing.

"Agreed," Werner panted.

A Violin's Secret

CHAPTER 5

W hen the first school bells sounded in town the next week, Werner and I walked along with very little talk, still thinking of our agreement not to tell my Father. Bruno, the town bully, saddled up beside us and palm popped me in the back of the head. I spun on Bruno with anger that cooled quickly knowing that Bruno could beat my head into different shapes.

"Hi Werner. Saw you running last week. How come you didn't invite me, instead of this one?" Bruno chided.

"Bruno, why do you always have to do that? You know I like Ernst. He doesn't bully others as you do," Werner complained.

"AaaaaHhhhh..." Bruno exclaimed as he ran ahead.

"Sorry, Ernst," Werner said.

"I don't like him and I can't see how you do," I said.

"I don't. I tolerate him because my father says to keep your enemies closer than your friends," he replied.

"What's that supposed to mean? Sounds dumb,"

"You'll see in the future," Werner looked toward the entrance of the schoolhouse. Werner should know since he was almost 15 years old.

We took our seats for the new school year where our new teacher, Miss Paget, sat us. I couldn't have cared where she sat me other than the back since I instantly feel for her night-black hair with those chocolaty eyes that always seemed to charm the boys in class into quiet submission. She didn't seem to work hard to keep the children in line since her looks garnered attention, and her gentle but authoritative words added the modicum of respect from others. She had my full admiration. The day's learning were best when she lectured, and we could soak in her beauty and wisdom at the same time.

I never remembered drifting off to day dream during her teachings. She always sought our learned opinions as well as questions as long as they had some consideration behind the statement or questions. The *Why* questions were not answered unless the student asked the question with additional pertinent details. I gleaned wisdom from her lectures every day and was allowed to think about my own views on the subject which made it so fun for me to be in her classroom. Even the loud and opinionated Bruno was relatively quiet.

Because Miss Paget was also a pianist, she taught music appreciation. We listened to phonographs of all great composers, especially Bach and Beethoven. We learned about their histories and their lives as well as why they wrote their music. When we came to Richard Wagner, Miss Paget would rush by his works without the flair that she taught with other composers. I asked her one time to explain why she didn't seem comfortable with Richard Wagner's life and works.

She told me that he had different views of the world and would not explain more. Querying my father about Wagner, he stated emphatically that Wagner had views that were more like Heir Hitler than with Christian teachings, and that I shouldn't mention Wagner's name in his presence again.

One Tuesday in late September, we noticed a younger student than me who came into class and was very nervous acting. Miss Paget took great care to give a hug to this child and make him feel welcome like few others. He was brown haired with a slightly darker complexion than most Aryans we had seen who scanned the room with furtive eyes waiting for the town bully to pounce. I had seen that same reaction in me with Bruno. While something made me feel sorry for the child for the way he would look around, I became jealous of the attention that Miss Paget paid him. How could I secretly run him away from my true love without her seeing what I was doing? I never seemed to think of a good way and told no one of this desire.

On Saturday afternoon, Werner and I walked to my home from school, partly to shield me from Bruno's verbal assaults which could come without Werner around. I flung open the door not fully grabbing a hold of it from a brisk wind as it banged against the wall to find a man, woman and that boy at the kitchen table. My father had his hand on the shoulder of the man with my mother's arm around the interloper seemingly comforting him. Tears were running down the woman's face, while the man's face looked downcast. I had seen that same expression on the people that moved to our town from the bigger cities all around Germany. It seemed all who came from the cities were hiding from a monster that they greatly feared, which was always written on their faces with worry-lines. And now my father started to wear the same look.

"Werner, go home," my father calmly stated.

"Yes, sir," as Werner pulled the door quickly shut behind him.

"Please come here, son. These people, Mr. and Mrs. Fagan with their son Vonn, are our *cousins*, and will be living with us for a while. They will move into your room, and you and Vonn will stay in your sister's room." My father had a strange look that I correctly took as one that meant that I should not test him regarding this new inconvenience. Unfortunately, I didn't stop myself in time for one question.

"But father, you have never told me of any cousins named the Fagan's; I've never seen them before!" Only later that night, I realized with regret, that I should have never asked the question with such a challenging tone. That comment bolted each adult in the room upright with a fleeting moment of panic.

"You must not have remembered. Take Vonn to your new room," father mumbled without challenging me back.

"Yes, Father," as I walked toward my little sister's room then turning to Vonn with a level of annoyance as if to say *hurry, and follow me, little irritant.* Vonn dutifully rose with only a glance toward his parents silently screaming his terror of this new surrounding.

I first stopped in my room with my mother right behind moving my clothes and music stand to my sister's room. When Katrina was told, she reacted with delight at the thought of two boys moving into her room, since it was the perfect excuse to require playing in her four-year-old fantasy world. I tried not to play with her unless I was directed to by my parents on occasion.

Vonn interestingly slipped to the floor beside her with no joy on his face to join her in looking at her dolls arranged in a semi-circle around her. Katrina began the doll introductions that gave me my clue to stop listening to her sing-song recitations. Fascinatingly, Vonn listened and never interrupted her while she listed her doll's names and fanciful histories for time until a thankful end. It was then that Vonn moved up in my book one notch only, because he was the perfect distraction for a little girl's ravings to allow me to escape. But, I vowed not to forget his unwitting betrayal of stealing any attention from my true love over that past two days at school.

The next day Vonn walked with me on the way to school in complete silence which made it seem like he wasn't even there, other than his boots crunching the frosted dirt path in early October. Werner moved quickly to take his usual place by me coming to school and paced by Vonn.

"So, who is this?" Werner questioned Vonn.

"His name is Vonn. He doesn't talk that much. He's my cousin," I said unconvincingly even to myself.

"Never met this cousin," Werner kindly looked down on Vonn.

"I know, I haven't either until my father introduced us last night. He and his family are going to stay with us for a while."

"Well, good. You can walk with us to school," Werner invited to get some type of response out of Vonn. All Werner received from Vonn was a slightly sad but hopeful look begging for a modicum of acceptance.

A dirt clod splattered against Vonn's brown coat. Some of the dirt spat up into my face. Vonn turned with a new look of terror as if he was having a continual nightmare that he had lived through many times before. His right eye winked closed waiting for the torrent of abuse without defending himself. I, on the other hand, hate-stared back at a deviously grinning Bruno four paces behind us. Bruno seemed to know that I would do nothing about the assault since I was too paralyzed by him. Werner did the opposite with a fire in his eyes that I couldn't remember before seeing.

"Bruno! Apologize to them right now!" Werner exclaimed with the authority only a teacher or parent could use.

"Ahh, I was just playing with them. They know it," Bruno wiped a crestfallen look off his face to replace it with surrender.

"Do it!"

"OK...sorrrryyy..." muttered Bruno as he pushed by trying to act as if he hadn't been scolded.

Werner brushed the dirt remnants off of Vonn's hair and coat while smiling down upon him. Vonn stared at Werner with a look of worship usually reserved for fathers. That day,

Vonn walked with his *Hero* and I to and from school. Werner never seemed to mind that Vonn would hardly walk out our front door or outside of the schoolhouse without him. Werner took the worship as an older brother would. This sibling protection forced me to drop my silly irritation with Vonn, of which he seemed to notice at first that I had something against him. Vonn, at first, didn't place the trust he had in me like he quickly developed for Werner.

Soon enough though, I began to coax Vonn to come outside with me after our chores were done to listen to me play my violin in the trees. He and the trees became my audience. Vonn would never talk much, but my music seemed to soothe and relax his shoulders while he played with the brittle grass of a fast approaching winter in 1942. I would play him every tune I knew and every variation of a tune I could. When I asked him how he liked them, a toothy smile met me like applause would a stage performer to which I would bow respectfully. As I played, I tended to think about things in the town, with the family living with us, and especially my love. Of course, I would never say anything but I would play for her, if not in person, but out here where God and all else could hear. Unfortunately, I mused that only Vonn heard my love songs. Until Bruno came by our clearing, which caused a very discordant sound off of my bow.

"Who *is* this kid? You know that the Gestapo has to be told of all people living here. There are rules that all people who move in to Ulm must register. I'll bet they haven't registered this child.

Whaddaya say, kid? Have you registered?" Bruno began to haul Vonn to his feet by his shirt collar.

"Would you leave him alone! He hasn't done anything to you!" I said suddenly grew a backbone.

"It is the duty of all good Germans to report things they see!"

"What do you need to report?" I demanded him to prove.

"I don't know. Just don't know why you are so jittery," pointing to Vonn after he released his horse-collar grip.

"I'll call for my father to make you leave," I used my violin's bow to extend a menacing pointer toward Bruno which made him shrink just a little.

"I'm goin', I'm goin'. But remember this, you have no real friends. Only good Germans have real friends. I *will* tell on you!" Since he had been able to bully a smaller person, Bruno slinked away toward his house closer to town. It made me suspicious since he lived nowhere close to my house, and I couldn't tell why he had been here.

"Don't worry about him, Vonn. He's harmless and a bully," I blathered very unconvincingly. Vonn just sat on shaking as fully as the grass was dying in the wind. He didn't get up to leave, but his eyes darted about as though looking for an escape.

That night, I told my father about this incident with Bruno. "That Bruno could be a problem," he reported to my mother.

Mr. Fagan started to say something to father until he placed his hand on Mr. Fagan's forearm. "I won't let anyone know," my father consoled.

Mr. Fagan then closed his mouth and masticated his butter and salted potato slowly. His wife peered alternately between her husband and her plate as the light outside began to darken. As much as the mood began to shadow the room as well, I was totally baffled by my father's reactions to Bruno. I hoped that he would punch Bruno for me, but that didn't seem to be the response I was getting from him. Concern for our family washed over his features. Besides, my father wouldn't have hurt Bruno for me anyway. He liked the saying of *turn the other cheek*. My problem was that both cheeks were red and blistered all the time by Bruno.

"Do I say anything to Bruno, father?"

"No! I will deal with it myself. You had better be careful not to anger him anymore. There is too much at stake," father chided me.

"But father, I did nothing but protect Vonn's feelings from a bully like you have always taught me to do without fighting?"

"I know, Son. But in these days, we cannot bring the town's attention upon us without hurting those we love," father explained knowing I didn't understand his meaning except that his jaw jetted toward our *cousins.*

Because we were so afraid of father's warnings regarding Bruno, we left very early on that Monday morning. Vonn and I walked cautiously as we scanned for Bruno with every step. It seemed that was a good idea since we missed most of my classmates as well as Vonn's Hero. As we approached the schoolhouse, I saw a military truck outside with only a driver and two soldiers standing by it.

In the past few years, most people learned never to look at soldiers as they did their business. We were told that soldiers had the right to protect Germany as needed, so Vonn and I looked down as we started to open the schoolhouse door. The door pushed back against my grip with more force than I applied to it as two more soldiers pushed it with Miss Paget's elbows being held in both men's hands. She had a pained expression. It was then that I noticed Mr. Reinholdt, the local Innkeeper who had lived in Ulm for the past five years. Mr. Reinholdt was sitting in the back of the truck that I hasn't looked in as I passed it. Their eyes met each other with a look of worry for one another more than for themselves.

"I told you that you don't need my fiancée! She has done nothing wrong. She is a good German teacher. Just take *me!*" he cried to the driver, who I then noticed wasn't the driver but had lieutenant bars on his collar.

"You both are to be taken for questioning. The children of Germany will be safe from the two of you," the last comment was spoken in the direction of Vonn and me. The security the lieutenant referred to had the opposite reaction than what he had hoped.

"Miss Paget, No! Don't take her!" I yelled while pulling the back of the truck.

One of the guards took a position between Miss Paget and me, while the other pushed me back five feet until I hit the muddy cobblestone still wet from the rainfall from the night before. Tears filled both of our eyes as they shoved Miss Paget into the truck. Mr. Reinholdt moved to her but could do little to help her up with his hands cuffed behind his back.

"Miss Paget!?" I cried after her.

"Take care of yourselves and your family. I will return to teach you more. It will only be a little while," sweetly her words tried to soothe both Vonn's and my tears. I noticed that tears were forming in her eyes as she sat back in the truck with a guard beside both of them. The lieutenant hopped into the passenger seat with the last guard getting into the driver's seat. The truck lurched as the guard ground the truck's transmission into first gear. I sat on that wet and muddy cobblestone for what seemed an eternity, while the sobs of Vonn replaced the sounds of the fleeting truck dropped off with a Doppler effect.

A Violin's Secret

CHAPTER 6

"Ernst! Ernst! What happened to the both of you?" Werner bent at the knees with his hand on my shoulder trying to shake me out of a tortured revere.

"They took her away," I blurted through my tears and mucous.

"Took who away?"

"They took Miss Paget and Mr. Reinholdt away!" I angrily yelled back at him.

"Who took them?"

"Soldiers came to the school as we were trying to beat Bruno here this morning. They took both of them away,"

"Why would they take her away?" Werner asked.

"She's his fiancée," I stated quieter now. Suddenly, the reality of my words hit me. She was engaged to him...to Mr. Reinholdt. I was torn with the emotions of her being taken away like I had seen some in our town taken. None ever returned but I had never really thought about it until that moment. I was also betrayed by Mr. Reinholdt who stood between my love as well.

"How could they do that?" I asked about both the engagement as well as the arrest with the same question.

"My father has told me that Mr. Reinholdt had been taking in *undesirables*. I didn't know that it applied to her?" Werner explained if that made sense to me. It seemed to startle Vonn though.

"Whaddaya mean *undesirables*?"

"You know. Those that the Fatherland doesn't want or need...the *Jews* to mention a few," he stated matter-of-factly.

"*The Jews*?" I stated knowing the race qualifier but not the word as Werner used it as if all Germany knew what he meant.

"The Jews are what's wrong with our world. Don't you know that? I've never met one myself, but my father tells me they took his father's business years ago. He says they are rats and carry diseases," Werner lectured. I was in no place to argue since I had heard none of what he was saying before. I also had never met a Jew.

"If he was hiding Jews, I am glad they took him away. It is sad that Miss Paget had to get involved with him. But, if she knew, she needs to be punished as well," again the matter-of-fact nature to his comments made it seem as if he were reading a textbook recitation.

"She was good!" I protested.

"Not if she helped that *Jew Lover*!" Werner shot back with a strong look of accusation.

"How do you know that she was a *Jew Lover*?" I pushed him back with my words without knowing what it really meant to be a Jew Lover.

Werner stood up and walked inside without answering my question. I also walked inside and took the hand of Vonn who was then terribly shaken.

As much of the class arrived within the next fifteen minutes, Mr. Heinz, who was the mayor of Ulm, announced to the class while writing on the chalkboard, "Miss Paget has been replaced this morning. Go home today and come back tomorrow. Her replacement will be here from Augsburg in the morning. Some real teaching will occur then, you'll see. She is *much* better than the *Jew Lover,* and you'll forget about her soon enough," he then started to dismiss the front rows of children moving toward the back of the class.

I was too stunned to say anything with the trauma of the morning burning a foreboding in my belly. So I led Vonn out of the schoolroom with the other children who were muttering to one another. No one else seemed to know why she had left, other than Werner and me. I stared off in the distance as I crossed the cobblestone to the other side of the street when a familiar voice sounded.

"She got what she deserved, you know," Bruno stood cross armed.

"What?" I muttered since I didn't hear him.

"I told them he was hiding Jews. I heard him say that he had found many in town who were hiding Jews with him. I thought that the *Sweet* Paget was in on it, too. They'll get theirs!" he burned with anger staring in the direction that the truck drove away.

"You? You turned them in, didn't you? I could kill you!"

"Yeah, you and how many of your Juden rats? I signed up this morning and was accepted with my act of bravery. I am sixteen and ready to be a real German," Bruno beamed at me.

46

I fought for composure and to keep from wanting to punch him. In seconds, my senses returned to the reality of a beating I would receive from Bruno's huge hands. Even though he was a bully and a coward, I had never really dared to take on his size. It scared me. Bruno must have sensed my fury and hatred.

"Careful, boy! Wouldn't want to bloody that nose. I could also report you as well..." he turned on his heels and headed toward town.

My anger quickly cooled as visions of being taken away like Mr. Reinholdt and Miss Paget flashed before my eyes. Without thinking of my direction, my feet pointed me toward the church. It was the one day of the week that my father worked at the church other than Sunday. I came in the church doors as if I was barging into my own house only to be scolded by my father as I moved down the aisle toward him.

"Could you give the house of the Lord some respect, Son?"

"Ohhh...I...I am sorry, father," I quickly apologized as I saw him near the piano in the church probably preparing for that coming Sunday as I tip-toed down the aisle. He said that it was easier to focus on the next Sunday's music needs when taking into consideration how the previous Sunday's response was to the music. He never told me who judged it, God or the parishioners. I know that he would pray about his music before and after the Sunday service. I always saw my father's image when I considered the term *devout*. My father finished touching up a piece at the piano and put his pencil down.

"What is the matter with you today, and why aren't you in school?" concern etched my father's brows.

"They arrested her!"

"Who did they arrest?"

"The police or army had lots of guards took my teacher away and Mr. Reinholdt. They said they were gone for good and that she wasn't going to teach in our school anymore!" I whimpered with tears starting to stain my high cheekbones. I could hear Vonn softly crying two pews back.

My father stood up and started to pace. Sometimes, when he said that he *had to think* he would pace or if he was concerned. His face showed a pale pink sinking in his cheeks. Father tugged at the top of his hair trying to figure some problem I wasn't privy to; I just hoped it was how to break Miss Paget out of jail.

"Did they say why she was taken away?" my father asked with great consternation in his voice.

"No, just that they were being talked to and that Germany was now safe."

"*Safe*? What did they mean by *safe*?"

"I do not know. They called her a *Jew Lover*."

"Did they see Vonn?" sudden alarm entered father's eyes without acknowledging the term.

"Yes. Why?"

"Oh my!" Father sighed and wiped his face in obvious frustration.

"What are we gonna do for Miss Paget? How do we get her out of jail? How do we get her away from Mr. Reinholdt since he did this to her?" I said in a rush.

"Wait a minute...Mr. Reinholdt and Miss Paget have both done some wonderful things together in the past several months to protect many families from the Gestapo. And why would you want her to get away from Mr. Reinholdt? He is a very good man, and I was going to play the *Wedding March* for them this spring."

"You knew they were getting married, father?" feeling betrayed by everyone in town now who knew of the *wedding* without thinking of my feelings.

"Yes. They told me about it three weeks ago but really didn't want the town to know about it since their activities to protect families are frowned upon by the authorities..." he trailed off in thought.

"If what they were doing was against the law, shouldn't he be punished?" my question unwittingly wanted him to be punished for his sins, not believing she was behind anything bad.

"There are times that governments make laws that are against the people whom they are supposed to protect. The book of Romans states clearly that we should uphold the laws of the land as long as they don't go against the laws of God," my father took a lecturing pose now.

"Well then, are the Jews like everyone else at school says they are and protecting them would make you a criminal?"

"The people that Germany are trying to hurt, by their new laws, are God's children, and they are definitely not criminals as the town is saying. Mr. Reinholdt and Miss Paget were protecting Jewish families that were going to be sent to those camps; I didn't want you to see when you asked about them a few months back," my father looked at me as if he knew that Werner and I had been to the camps, but I hoped that he was just lecturing and didn't really know what we had done. Thinking of those camps made me shiver some.

"Vonn and his family are those people we are protecting right now!" Father nodded toward Vonn who shied away now from our gaze.

I then turned to stared at Vonn as if for the first time. I looked at his brown eyes and his curly hair around his ears not even able to believe what my eyes were seeing for a Jewish boy.

At first, my brow furrowed in confusion thinking that he was the enemy again like when he was competing for Miss Paget's attention. Then, my heart softened when I thought of the troubled boy who only found moments of solace within my violin strings. I let the vision of the troubled boy win my heart over. I went to Vonn and put my hand on his right shoulder and nodded my approval of him: who he was and that he was good. For a long moment, he wouldn't meet my gaze. Slowly, he looked up and saw in my eyes, the concern of an older brother. From that point on, I decided that I would be this boy's older brother. Father then crossed in front of me and wrapped both of us in his arms. Vonn's tears bled into father's tweed coat as well as my continued questions about the bad man I thought Mr. Reinholdt to be, except for one.

"Can we rescue them from the guards?" I muffled into his chest.

Then my father crushed my hopes with a pat on my head. While Vonn's tears were being dried on Father's coat, I began to stain it again with my own. I then realized she was more than gone to my heart, but the deeper meaning to be gone forever. I then prayed that God would wrap Himself around her for protection. Vonn and I made our way back to the house where I told my mother and the Fagan's the whole morning's story. Then Mrs. Fagan began to pace the floor. She picked up my mother's pans and polished them as if they were the dirtiest things on earth. Mr. Fagan went outside and began chopping wood frantically. They seemed so broken for my loss it brought me closer to them. At least that is what I thought they felt. That night my parents filled me in on the details as to Vonn's past.

CHAPTER 7

Vonn was born in Augsburg in a happy home with loving parents and grandparents. His grandparents and parents didn't have a financial standing within the community, but they took joy swinging their grandson in the park. Mr. Fagan worked as a baker making fine breads until one day he was fired because of his Jewish roots. When his town understood his family tree, he couldn't work anywhere but in the Jewish quarters of the city. His father began to walk down dirty avenues kicking empty beer bottles rather than the river rocks in the park. But when his family took their daily jaunts, they were free again. His father had told Vonn that walking was one thing that they couldn't take away from them no matter where they had to live or work. That is when the itinerant lifestyle began for Vonn. School was low on the priority pole. Food and shelter were hard to find especially when they moved from place to place. Each room was smaller and took several days or weeks to procure a new domicile, since all of the locales were crowded with less square footage and more frantic populations of Jews being forced into restricted areas of the city.

As the trains came for deportation to the East (no one ever was told exactly where they went), the Fagan's stole away in the night with a few knapsacks of food and one extra pair of clothing. His grandparents gave them all they had to barter and trade so that they could make it out. Vonn cried for hours silently on his father's shoulder as they left the city away from his beloved grandparents. They traversed through the country side staying close to the river Danube for possibilities of water and food. With many trees lining the Danube, shelter was a lean-to against a tree. Mr. Fagan put a bright face on the circumstances for Vonn saying that they were camping out across Germany to see the countryside. Vonn began to see it as a wonderful time without dirty looks from the Aryans who spit in his direction within the city. A few farms along the way allowed them to stay in their barns until they met Miss Paget in Ulm.

Miss Paget took them in on the outskirts of her town, settling them in Mr. Reinhold's Inn. Every day after her teaching, Miss Paget and Mr. Reinholdt brought them food and newer clothing. They cut Mr. Fagan's hair and beard as well as colored them with bleach a slightly lighter pigment hoping to blend more into Ulm. After a few weeks with a bed and mostly enough to eat, Mr. Reinholdt brought my father by to meet this family. My father even admitted, shamefully he added, that he was very reluctant to take a Jewish family in.

"If they are caught, we also pay the price," my father had said almost to himself as much as to Mr. Reinholdt.

"I know, and the Lord won't be angry if you don't want to take them in. But....many families around town are doing this same thing. No one knows one another and are disguised. You won't know them and they won't know you," Mr. Reinholdt pleaded with my father, in the most gentle fashion, to help. But as I heard the story, I knew my father needed very little pleading since there was only one choice a good man like my father would make.

I was told this in the strictest of confidence, as Vonn stared into the light of the candle not really transfixed by the story but potentially lost in the song of a violin, I mused. For my part, I promised with my life, to the Fagan's, that I would protect Vonn as well as never say a word. My mother kissed my head in approval for my vow as my father beamed a pride that put the huge candle's light to shame. My father's pride in me was evident that night which strengthened my resolve to take an active role in resistance.

Of course, all of us in Ulm had read the signs condemning the Jews for everything that was bad in Germany including any hardship that the war squeezed on the loyal citizens. Then I realized that my country was wrong about the Jews and Mr. Reinholdt was a man to be looked up to as highly as my father. This only made my heart ache more for my teacher and for her protection.

The next morning, Vonn and I took careful steps in the morning toward the school. I realized that I was a spy, and I was then an enemy of Germany if anyone found out who Vonn was. I pondered the story during the last night as we walked so early in the morning.

For the first time I then began to pray, and I realized that morning was the day I became a man when I began to supplicate for someone other than myself. In the past, I prayed for God to make Bruno leave me alone; to have a better violin; or to make me noticeable to Miss Paget. In the space of one day, I voiced concern for Vonn and his family's safety, and that my path to and from school would take us out of harm's way. I put my arm around his shoulder as we walked and he leaned toward me, too.

Inside the school, we met our new teacher who seemed to glower with every glance. The head tilt aimed at a child extracted any ounce of self-pride. We were to be clay jars for her to break and remold into a new pot she called Patriotic Germans.

"Good morning, class. I am Mrs. Gerhardt. I am your new instructor. I have been told of the ease of your teaching schedule as well as the lax in discipline that the Fuhrer demands of all children of the glorious *Third Reich!*" she yelled. We were so taken aback that we sat as far back in our seats as we coul,d while Bruno brought himself to his feet.

"Heil, Hitler!" Bruno screamed with a crack of his voice into a slight falsetto.

"Heil, Hitler, children! You all will rise to speak it, too!" She demanded in response.

The class bolted upon their feet as she asked three times until the screams were at a sufficient volume to allow us to seat ourselves again. Children in the front row, like Vonn, spoke the words without knowing the depth of their spiritual resonance, while the teenagers in the back of the class screamed it with a fervor I had rarely heard. I spoke in a whisper since I knew a little of what it really meant, other than a feeling in my soul that it must be something wrong.

"Today, we will learn about how the Jews have slaughtered good Germans during the last war. Later in the afternoon, we will listen to our Fuhrer's favorite composer, Richard Wagner, as you work on your math. After school, those thirteen years and older will stay to form Ulm's first Hitler's Youth. I am ashamed to say that the school's greatest duty in making young girls and boys into functioning adults has been frittered away without the formation in our school of a good Hitler Youth program. I will remedy this today!" she bellowed as she started spitting venom about the rats called Jews. Vonn shrank into his seat which seemed to be close to how the other younger children sat in their chairs this morning with the booming voice of intimidation that fueled Mrs. Gerhardt's raged.

Even though I tried to be a man that father would be proud of for not crying in public, it seemed to take all my effort not to do so. I could only look down at the homework and try to focus upon it. Mrs. Gerhardt walked by each desk and corrected in a loud voice, mostly in discouraging words and sighs of frustration, at our lack of mental production. She only nodded her head as she walked by my desk. The other children were very distracted by her presence, but the homework helped me not to think of the new realities: no more kind words from Miss Paget.

Mrs. Gerhardt was 5'7" and seemed to be nearly as wide as she was tall. She seemingly had arms of steel which were not out of place when thinking of her girth. There was always a continual scowl forming near her black eye brows. When her head moved from child to child, watching for any *malcontent behaviors*, as she would put it, her black hair would not move within the tightly woven bun at the back of her head. She didn't have the flowing hair of Miss Paget, more like something painted on by the costume designers in a play.

As day went into day of that first week during the reign of Mrs. Gerhardt, her dress style never changed. It was the white blouse and black skirts. Never did I see her smile outside of the droning of Wagner. Vonn held his stomach as we walked to and from school probably unclenching his gut since Mrs. Gerhardt seemed to delight in frightening the smaller ones in class. Vonn's fear caused her to lift a corner of her mouth in what some would consider a smirk; I just knew she was evil since she had replaced *my* love.

The only thing that calmed Vonn down was our afternoon music time for which he would plead. But I was not in the mood to play anything bright and cheery on any of those afternoons. My music was darker than rumbling, major keys of Wagner. Even though Wagner's music was technically brilliant, his writings, my father told me on one Sunday afternoon, talked of how Jews were the dogs of society and only the Aryan Germanic race was superior. If I had heard these concepts several months earlier before I had met the Fagan's, I would have possibly believed it. I even asked father about my doubt of God.

"Why does God let bad things happen like what you told me of Vonn's family?" I asked father as I helped him clean his shop after school one day.

"Well...God doesn't like the things that men do. It utterly grieves Him, but He allows bad things because of the sinfulness of the world."

"Then He could take away that sin, so that Vonn's family would be safe again," I reasoned.

"Wish it worked that way. You see, if He took away someone's ability to sin, He would take away our choices. If we had no choices, we would *have* to do what He says. That would be no world to live in and no one would really love Him," my father seemed to explain things in ways I could understand.

"But why doesn't everyone choose to be nice to the Jews? Why can't people just leave them alone? I don't understand Mrs. Gerhardt, and what she says about Wagner and the Fuhrer report about the Jews! Vonn is a good little guy, don't you think, Father?"

"Yes, he is and his family is, too. Germany is experiencing a dark period. Hatred of Jews is only a symptom of a deeper problem. We have forgotten that the Bible calls the Jews God's chosen people. Abraham was told that 'those who bless thee, will be blessed, and those who curse thee, will be cursed.'"

"So Germany is being cursed?"

"The war has gone on now for a several years. I fear that with the Americans and the Russians fighting us, we will lose. We will pay for our arrogance. But I want to stand before the Lord knowing I did the right thing, that I stood up for those who were being persecuted like the Good

Book says to do," my father proclaimed. In that moment, I was never more proud to be his son.

"Ernst, you have to be very careful in the days ahead. We are heading toward 1943, and I fear that bad things will be headed for our town. Always be watching for those who would hear what you say in private. Miss Paget was taken away, because she did the right thing. God never said that we would not suffer; He did say that we *would*. Do not speak of this to the Fagan's or to anyone at school."

This statement startled me. I began to frantically search my memory for any time that I might have casually spoken of our family's faith or our family's secret of the Fagan's. I inwardly cursed myself for even the possible hint of me telling anyone anything that might give us away, even though I couldn't conceive of any potential incident. I could never let my father down by being so stupid as to say something to the wrong person.

That night I was more silent at the dinner table, contemplating the depth of my parent's secret. To my amazement and their credit, they showed nothing of the burden they carried. Smiles and greetings at the dinner table kept up while my bad mood deepened. My mother seemed to know how I was feeling and would wink at me every now and then during supper, trying to lift my spirits. I was unsure if my spirit would ever fly again.

Going to school on another Monday morning, Vonn's shoulders slumped even farther than usual. Every time I asked him how he was feeling, he non-verbally responded with a shrugging of those shoulders forward. Bruno was waiting near the school room doors looking for us as I quickly tried to move passed him into the school house.

"What's your hurry?" he stepped into my path. I noticed an armband of black around his right bicep.

"What is the armband for?" I tried to dissuade him from bothering me or Vonn by faking an interest in him.

"It's my new rank," he raised his nose a little higher with pride. "I am a sergeant in Ulm's Nazi Youth from Colonel Gerhardt. The Colonel says I have high leadership potential and has given my name to the S.S. She knows military talent when she sees it since her husband is fighting on the Eastern Front against the Bolshevik Swine."

"Wow, you must be proud," I feigned admiration.

"You bet I am. I want to be like my father who is in a tank division in France. He is a Captain who drove the Brits out of Dunkirk. They'll never stand a chance against men like him. My father wrote me and told me that it was my duty to sign up for the Wehrmacht. I would have done so next month if it weren't for Colonel telling me that I had the makings of a good S.S. agent. It was some of my information that led to the arrest of the criminals we used to call our teacher, you remember her, don't you?"

"Yes, that was great," I muttered trying to move past him.

"Maybe you can be my volunteer private, Ernst, and raise your position in my eyes?" he questioned conspiratorially.

"Maybe?"

"There are still stinking Jews in Ulm. While I heard that they broke Miss Paget and her traitor pig fiancée into admitting that they had hidden some Jews, they never got any names of the traitors to Germany. Do you know who those might be? I could make it worth your while?" Bruno winked.

"I...uh...don't...I know that I don't..." I looked at him with a stunned expression. Vonn's face went pale and panic brought a tear to the corner of his right eye. I prayed that an angel might smite Bruno down or take me away on a chariot; either way I would be out of a situation I felt that I didn't have the ability to bear.

"If you do, I could make you a corporal," he winked again and let me pass as I sat in my assigned seat. Vonn never seemed to get the rosy color to come back to his cheeks that day while I spoke not a word for minutes as the class filled up.

"How are you doing today on this fine day with the Fuhrer shining down on us, Ernst?" Werner beamed. I saw the same uniform that Bruno wore which was so striking in contrast to the bright colors he normally wore. The uniform was a light brown shirt with long knickers and high black socks. His boots were spit-polished black. He had an insignia with two more stripes on his collar than Bruno's.

"What does that signify?" I pointed to his collar.

"I am Ulm's first Lieutenant in the Nazi Youth! My father would be so proud if he were still here," he lifted his collar toward me with a wistful look.

Last year, his family had received a letter from the government saying that his father had died on the Eastern Front while pushing toward Belarus, Soviet Union. In June of 1941, Germany had decided to break their pact with Stalin and invade Russia. They moved through the country side quickly while running into farming communities similar to Western Germany's lands which they burned to the ground. Werner's father reported to his family through letters, which were heavily censored, that the Soviets were brutal to their own land and people. Werner's father wrote that he hated them more every day he was in their country. His father sent letters to Werner that he would read to me about their exploits saying that they would be in Moscow within November 1941. The letters stopped for three weeks before his mother was told that he had been killed outside of Belarus. Werner tried to not grieve too much as people around town congratulated him for being the son of a war hero. I saw the tears fall only a few times while his jaws clenched every time someone said anything about his father. This type of painful glory was Germany's lot for those who believed in the Fuhrer. My father was one of those who taught us to be wary of this greed for territory that the military sowed in this time. I was so grateful that my father was deemed too important to the war effort at home with his carpentry skills to be sent to battle.

We started that day, the same way we ended school with too much of Mrs. Gerhardt's yelling and no quiet learning. I started to believe that this was what it was like to be in the Wehrmacht. This is the life that Bruno and

Werner were heading towards as well as me when I was just one year older. I acted in class as if bombs were dropping around me every time our new teacher yelled a lesson. My eyelashes would flutter shut; more so as she would walk toward my desk. Most of the front row still pulled back in terror while the back rows with the older teen's chairs screeched in excitement with *Heil Hitler* on the teen's lips and hands in salute.

At times the cacophony would reach a fevered pitch in which the back rows roared forcing all "good German children" to rise to their feet and claim victory for the Fuhrer, if that were possible from our little school room that and the world was listening. All of us were required to agree with these displays, with forcible encouragements from the older ones. I would stand up but many times I would drop my chalk hoping I wasn't seen praising a Fuhrer my father was showing me was bad for Germany. Only inside my house were we able to show our true feelings; outside the danger of letting one's personal feelings out bought you a ride in a truck away from your family with two S.S. guards at your side. *Thank God*, I thought that most of my class didn't notice my lack of displays of affection for the Fuhrer. *Thank God indeed.*

CHAPTER 8

As winter grew more harsh in Ulm, most outdoor activities died down. A smile seemed to break our moods with Christmas approaching on December 23, 1942. I had carved wood sculptures of my family for each member including Uncle and Aunt Fagan, as we now referred to them in private as well as public situations. My father's work as a carpenter was slowly losing its money stream with so few people needing new furniture. The war was center stage on everyone's mind, except my father, had dodged entry into it with his necessary labor as one of the town's few carpenters left, since the war took the rest of them. My father was busy with the town's carpentry chores without much ability for the people to pay him. There were repairs from the bombings that would rattle everyone who lived inside the town's limits as well as holes in the walls that he was required to do on orders from Ulm's town government.

The bigger concern for me was the darkness that came over even our family discussions at home. More fervent prayer for those in need as well as protection for us against a future my parents suspected but wouldn't let me in on. I could sense a danger with the changes within the school as well as the changes in the town's folk, but I was never really able to grasp the magnitude of what I heard in my parent's prayers after I was ordered to bed nightly. They were worried about an *enemy coming* (the only thing I could hear through the bedroom walls).

I never tried to pass on my growing concern toward Vonn or my sister. I didn't want them to worry, but I could tell they were. I would wink at Vonn if he looked my way in bed only slightly diverting my attention away from the listening forays through the walls. Once I heard them talk of neighbors who were taken away, but I couldn't make out the names. I would even dream of those neighbors who were forced into a truck as Miss Paget was. Sometimes, my night terrors would transpose me into the neighbor's fate, and I would wake in a panic.

On Christmas day, we saw the tree decorated the night before with a few gifts upon it. I received clean sheets music on which I could compose. I was so excited about this possibility of composing even though it terrified me to consider writing. The terror and excitement must have looked the same on my face, about which gave the adults joy thinking I loved the gift. While I did love it, I had a belief that no one could like *my own* music. Sure, they could listen me play other's pieces but one of my own pieces was beyond my imagination. I took the sheets later that day as a sign from God that I needed to make my life goal that of being a great songwriter, and I prayed He would imbue me with that gift.

My first few songs were so bad that I scribbled them away. I kept a few of the progressions through which lead to my first real song called

Promise. It was filled with an uplifting melody that was played in the key of C. I then wrote several days later, *Roses,* of which I had significant trouble in connecting the two melodies since I had wanted the second to be a movement flowing nicely from the first.

My father seemed delighted on a late Sunday afternoon to stay longer within the church to pound out the transitions between the two movements. He would even play along and Vonn would linger between the two instruments bobbing his head and rhythmically swaying to the music. Father would nod his head in the direction of Vonn with a smile to get my attention of which I turned the instrument in his direction as if to serenade him. As we played it further my father would say, "What about this?" or "Could we try this?" to create the flow we were looking for. It was one of the first times which my father and I were truly communicating without words. Music allowed us to connect without utterances by the notes and head bobs to signal changes the other might follow. The rapturous feelings tingled my skin. This is what I wanted to do with my life. I wanted harmonies to move inside of minor chords that the piano seemed to love. My violin was reborn for minor keys, as I hoped that I was interpreting its responses to the notes I played upon it. Outwardly though, our country was singing on a decidedly discordant key. I didn't want it to be a reflection of my soul and my music to the Lord, or for that dissonance to break ties with my father's piano.

When it came to the school, I kept my head down but my mind on my music. It didn't seem as bad as I once felt it to be within the town, even though Bruno and Werner spent most of their time drilling in the streets in front of the school house in the evening. Vonn and I would walk the longest route around them so as not to arouse suspicion. Werner must have noticed; Bruno watched everything that Werner did. So Bruno and Werner must have sensed something was different within me. I suspected that there was a spirit empowering the two of them in kinship for a sickening cause against me. They drilled and yelled *Heil Hitler* until the crackling of their voices were heard far down the street, with the chorus chasing me home.

During the next few weeks into early 1943, my father seemed to love our playing as well since it was our expression of gratitude toward each other as well as to the Lord who carried us through another day. Vonn, on the other hand, didn't seem to experience any conscious thought while listening to us play soothing his soul. The rehearsals, as I called it, only could happen on Sundays through Tuesdays since my father was too busy doing carpentry for the city. He was paid little for it, but we were allowed a few extra rations *under the table* as he called it by those people whose rooms he fixed.

During one day in late February 1943, our teacher required the pledge to the Fuhrer as she had done before. I didn't even think about it this day since I was considering what my father and I were going to play that Tuesday after school. I usually spoke the Lord's Prayer that my father had taught me with a whisper cadence to the pledge. It was my form of resistance that my father practiced outwardly against the wrongdoings of our nation and its pitiful new rules against anyone who wasn't Aryan, that is, blue eyed and blonde haired without a trace of Jewish or Slavic blood.

I could blend in since I looked the part as did many of the children, but it seemed that it wasn't enough to act the part; one must play it with heart. I understood the difference better than most of the other children since I was a musician. Notes played without heart were discordant. Music with passion, such as how my father and I played, changed the mood of the listener. Werner and Bruno spoke the Pledge as well as their *Heil Hitler's* with that same heart my father and I used, but with a disgusting anger behind it. I rarely spoke to either of them except when ordered to do so, which was their preferred communication these days. At times, from the corner of my left eye, I caught a frown from Bruno during his recitations for his fervor of Nazi ideas. I was never sure what my face was saying, but I feared that it was betraying me somehow. That Tuesday late afternoon would change the course of my life.

"Where are you goin'? The younger ones watch us and you...you *are* old enough to join the Hitler Youth!" Bruno barked as Vonn and I stepped out of the school house at the end of the day where he seemed to be waiting to ambush me.

"I didn't know that, Sir?" I responded as I looked down knowing that he wanted to be called *Sir* by his classmates..

"Today is your lucky day, recruit! I am taking new malcontents to my Captain and will give me a promotion with the next one for this month," Bruno pointed in the direction of Werner who had two bars on his collar, updating me to his new rank of First Lieutenant. Werner turned to us as he strode over to our spot among our classmates with an authority and an arrogance I had never seen in his eyes. I could hardly recognize him in the way he carried himself.

"Is there a problem, Lieutenant?" Werner ordered.

"No problem here, Sir. Just trying to recruit one who has been hanging upon the fringes of our society. I am not sure he understands Germany's fight within our borders as well as without, Sir," Bruno snapped to order in front of the *Captain.*

I had no idea about what he was speaking, although I knew he was nefariously discussing my fate if I choose against recruitment. My confusion was easy to see in the eyes of these two strangers I had grown up with my whole life.

"Well...what is your decision, recruit?" Werner snapped at me.

My mind went blank. I uttered with my lips a prayer.

"What was that recruit?" Bruno bellowed as he leaned in cupping his left ear.

"I need to ask my father first," I whispered.

"You don't have to ask *your father*! Any good German father's dream would be for his son to enter the Hitler Youth..."

"Lieutenant, allow the *boy* time to talk to his father," Werner said *boy* with contempt. As soon as he said that, he instantly softened with a slight sense of shame for putting down a friend of so many years. The *Captain* turned on his heels and began attending to new recruits of a younger age than I was.

"You have 48 hours to come back to sign up or I will *report you to the authorities*!" Bruno stated with disgust in my direction and turned his back toward another possible recruit to fill his ghastly quota.

Both Vonn and I were visibly shaken. I walked as quickly as possible in a route that would take us out of eye shot of the gathering, so that I could lean against a bakery and allow both of us to share a tear or two. Vonn took more than I felt his allotment should be but kept them silent. Within a few minutes we had composed ourselves enough to hurry to the church.

After I told my father the occurrence outside the school house, he was more shaken than I felt. He began to pace as he did on the day I told him about Miss Paget. Vonn moved to a side pew and brought every tear he could with silent convulsions. I sat heavily upon the piano bench where he played every Sunday so I could turn the pages for him. This seat used to be a place of rest, but I knew that there would be no more rest only the noise of Hitler.

"I guess the only thing left to us is pray that John 8 also occurs for us," father mused.

"What's John 8 say?"

"When Jesus was preaching, many didn't like what He was saying that He was the Messiah. He said that He was before Abraham. This didn't sit well with the many people of the day. As they tried to stone him, he slipped away."

"Are they going to stone us if I don't become one of the Hitler Youth? I'll do it to protect our family if you wish."

"No. Do what you know to be right."

"I don't want to join the Hitler Youth. I have seen the change in Werner; I don't want to become that," I said while my face masked disgust.

"That is correct, Ernst. Do not join. I pray that God will blind those eyes He needs to but we will follow him," my father's sermon was over as he sat at the piano. We watched the keyboard for several minutes without a word or a gesture.

"Let's get started. I have so enjoyed watching your skills grow as a violinist, Ernst. You are becoming quite good," he smiled halfheartedly trying to cheer me. When you are young, cheering from your father isn't that hard to accomplish.

"Yes, father. Where should we begin?"

He played into my songs and built more impromptu duets as we went. The songs didn't matter much as long as they were harmonies. I wanted to forget about the discordant sounds from in front of the school house. The piano did the trick for Vonn and me. Vonn laid his head back on the pew and closed his eyes. Within minutes, he fell asleep. We smiled again knowing that sleep was all he needed.

The next few months were spent in town and among others in relative quietness. I rarely spoke unless addressed to by anyone. I wasn't trying to be rude but to not be noticed so that I may slip out of circumstances that might be harmful much as Jesus did. I didn't believe I could be as Jesus was, but I prayed that He would make me less visible in this troubled time.

There was a good and bad thing about being purposely less visible in a town where everyone knows everyone else. The good was that due to the consternation upon people's faces because of the war, you were allowed to live your life in some solitude. The bad was that you constantly felt that people were talking about you if they ever looked in your direction. Bruno seemed to forget about the 48 hours. I felt that I was horrible at wearing my emotional state upon my face and everyone knew what I was worried about. One early April morning, I found out the truth.

A Violin's Secret

CHAPTER 9

Vonn and I purposefully walked to school as we had every morning in the least traveled routes. Many times they were also interesting routes since it took us by parts of town we didn't always see. The worsening conditions in Ulm was even evident upon the gaunt faces of the dogs in the streets without owners to care for them. They followed us many mornings for yards until it became apparent that we would provide them with no food. To my dismay, as we reached the outer doors of the school house, Bruno stood by it almost as though he was waiting for me. I tried to brush this thought aside since he didn't see me until we were near the portal.

"I've been looking for you," Bruno turned to me.

"Yes, Sir?" I chimed dutifully.

"Well...what have you chosen to do with my offer to be a private in Ulm's Hitler's Youth movement? We have lots of possibilities for advancement for the right prospects, you know..." he trailed off waiting for my response.

"Sir, I said that I was going to think about it..." I also hung the sentence without finishing it.

"Yeah, I know that. Enough thinking; more doing is what Colonel Gerhardt always says at our meetings. What'll it be?" Bruno leaned into me.

"I can't, sir," I said with a whisper.

"I better not have heard can't...do you really want to disappoint me?" now taking on an ominous tone while taking an intimidating step toward me to look down his nose.

"I cannot."

"You're not done with me, yet," Bruno turned on his heels as if he were a young boy out of options in the argument going to tattle on me. The reality of this view was that it was not a too distant fulfilled prophecy.

All that day, I saw kids in class than usual, looking in my direction as they spoke in whispered screams that never reached my ears. I pretended not to notice that they were talking about me as well as praying that they weren't. But as the day lingered far into the afternoon, it became apparent that even Werner was looking in my direction with a level of distain that I had never seen before; it was a look that would stay with me for years. That stare also symbolized for years of how I would see other Germans after the war when I thought about my experiences.

I walked home in utter fear that night and told my parents as well as the Fagan's what had occurred in school. I hoped that they would calm me but that never came. At night, my mother and Aunt cooked and baked as if the church was having their annual bake sale the next morning. Father and Uncle Fagan sorted then began to pack away clothes as if in preparation for a long winter storm rumoring to cut all power to the city.

At 6AM the next morning, a loud and impatient rapping was heard at our front door. I awoke to it with a start, but the door was opened quickly as if my parents were expecting the knock. A uniformed man stood in the door with a clipboard reading with little emotion in his voice his pronouncement we had dreaded:

"Are you the Huntelmann's?"

"Yes, we are, officer. What can we..." my father was cut off.

"You are hereby requested and required, along with your family to come with us for questioning to our headquarters. You are allowed one suitcase per person since it will be several days ride to headquarters. We will give you fifteen minutes to pack. If you are innocent, we will return you home. If not, this house will be repatriated," the officer almost with a yawn of boredom rattled off his sentence upon our family.

I looked around and found that my parents had somehow expected this but were still looking for valuable items that they needed for the trip. My mother herded us together. Vonn and I complied with some bewilderment, but Katrina started to cry when told that we were leaving for a while on a *trip*. She wanted to take all of her dolls that she showed Vonn on his first day but was finally allowed only one doll. This made the crying and angst even climb to a higher wail than normal pleading for Mother to bring more dolls. Father then stepped in with a command that stopped her wailing instantly into dulled tears. Without realizing it, I started to tear up. I then looked about the house, not realizing that it really would be the last time.

We were herded out of our own house by impatient guards. My violin in its case and a suitcase, that I struggled to move quickly enough, were thrown into the back of the truck along with a shove in my bottom upward toward a burlap smell; a smell that I would become all too familiar with in the years to come. It was musty from the rains from the night before, and the dew on it that was starting to dry in the morning sun. The sunshine that filled my eyes blotted the tears that fell more rapidly as I sat down in a seat toward the front of the truck. Around me were the Fagan's and my parents. Katrina was sitting on my mother's lap being comforted by her rocking motion. We were bounced throughout the town and could see little of where we were going from the back of the vehicle. I then realized that it had to be my fault for not accepting the offer to become a Hitler's Youth. If I had just accepted the evil invitation, I could have spared my family this heartache. I gritted my teeth and streamed regretful tears, while we ricocheted through the city to a larger road outside of town.

After two hours of riding, my sister had long since stretched out on my parents laps as did Vonn had on his parents. Many times dust filled the back of the truck when caravans of vehicles passed from the opposite direction. Almost in unison we would crane our necks as far forward as possible to miss the dirt that filled our lungs from each procession. We bounded into a smaller town with lots of barbed wire fences and rows of buildings about which my father asked of the guards if this was the headquarters. All he got as a response was one vertical head bob. As soon as the truck stopped, we were hurried from the truck with our belongings inside a near building. The place smelled so familiar with the camp that we had spied a year ago in the woods. We formed a line behind some ten other families all having the same sense of foreboding as well as confusion about the next step. We were told to wait in line for our turn.

"Our turn for what, father?," I asked the obvious.

"I don't think anyone will tell us until our turn comes. We will have to be patient," father nodded in the direction of the two younger ones. "You, Son, are going to have to grow up quickly now. I might not be able to answer any of your questions, and you will need to help us keep your sister and cousin from complaining too much. I don't think that they will have much patience for crying young ones. Trust in the Lord, and He will carry us through this. No matter what happens to your mother and me, watch out for the children. Try to stay together as much as possible. If we get separated..." my father trailed off trying choking a smile on the right corner of his mount for reassurance. It was amazing that a smile from your father could communicate so much of concern, reassurance, and pride. It was also equally disturbing to see the crack in the façade within a father's tone. I only nodded my head.

I knew that I would have to be the man of the family in some ways since my father was partially abdicating his authority. He must have sensed a problem growing out of his control, but I knew that even if he hadn't communicated the trouble we were in. I would have to carry the slack since I was to blame for our predicament. I got us arrested, and I vowed to become a man as well as not cry again like I had done in the truck.

We waited for hours and crept forward in line slowly. I heard a few shouts by guards and some plaintiff sounding voices sometimes in our language or sometimes in another languages coming from behind the door. Most of the time we could not hear the details of the conversation, but the tone was unmistakable with dread from the questioned trying to avoid the arrest, I supposed. We were called for and expected to move in with haste. My father and Mr. Fagan spoke for the family. I hardly heard what was being said because of my interminable guilt for my father to have to be subjected so. Mostly, they seemed to verify personal information about us when one of the interrogators, Long Nose, looked more closely at the papers and then scrutinized Mr. Fagan and his family. Long Nose ordered that the Fagan's step aside to look them over. Long Nose wanted to know their family background, and why their papers seemed to be out of order, which made no sense to me.

"I took my family out of Augsburg since there was so little work in the city. My cousin here was kind enough to take me in, and I worked with him in his shop as a carpenter. I am a good carpenter," Mr. Fagan cheerfully offered.

"But you look Jewish to me...your papers don't say anything about your rat heritage. Can you answer that, Juden?" Long Nose poked him in the chest.

"But Sir...my papers are clear that I am German born as well as my family all from Augsburg..." Mr. Fagan pleaded with Long Nose that was clearly not buying what Mr. Fagan was selling.

"You are...Juden Rat. I am trained to see you vermin from miles away. Are you saying that I am stupid?"

"No one is saying anything of the kind, sir," my father intruded. "What my *cousin* is saying is that the Glorious German conflict has made all good German's huddle together with some deprivation, so that we may be victorious in the end against our enemies. That is why he came to live with me..."

"Shut up, *pig.* If it is determined that this vermin is what I suppose, you will be in enough trouble for harboring criminals of the state," my father was backhanded for his diatribe creating a trickle of blood from his nose.

I moved forward about to interject that I was the cause for the arrest with my disobedience to not join the Hitler's Youth when ordered to do so. I would come clean and pronounce innocence for my family no matter the cost to me. Even if I had to work all day long in a camp like the one I saw beyond the forest that day with Werner which scared us so much, I was determined to pay the price for the Fagan's and us. My father quickly saw my intentions. He stopped me with an arm to my chest and a quick nod of his eyes to stay back. Long Nose didn't seem to notice any of our non-verbal exchange, but I stepped back behind my father.

"You know," Long Nose, who was obviously in charge of our future at this point, nodded toward his subordinate behind the desk who had barked some of the opening questions, "I think they are lying to me. I think that these three over here (pointing to the Fagan's) really are Jews. There is only one way to find out…" Long Nose grabbed Mr. Fagan's trousers and ripped them down until his private parts were exposed to the shock of both families. Both families jerked in reaction, mostly away from the horror of the violation to lessen Mr. Fagan's shame.

"See? Circumcised! That is the final evidence that even a court of law would convict. Take them ALL away," Long Nose barked an order to the guards behind us who jerked Mrs. Fagan out of her stupor while Mr. Fagan hurriedly pulled his pants up with both hands to cover himself from the indignity. One last guard tugged Vonn so hard by his left shoulder lifting him three inches off the ground until his feet started moving in the direction to the right down a long hallway to the outside.

"You…" Long Nose pointed with his riding whip I hadn't even seen that he had, "have now been proven an enemy of the state by harboring Jews. Even though your papers are in order and the Sergeant would have let you go, this evidence has proven your guilt as well."

Long Nose then spoke fateful words in which I had heard once before. Words that had chilled my fingers numb, "Germany needs to be kept safe from you. Deal with them, Sergeant." Long Nose tossed the words casually over his shoulder pronouncing our fate with his whip.

Within minutes we were processed in line in front of train tracks. Our bags had a *D* written upon them as well as a *D* was written on the front of each of my family's coats. Then we were told to wait for loading.

"What's the *D* stand for, Father," my sister asked.

"I don't know, honey. Be a good girl now and wait for a train ride to come and take us on a journey," my mother answered for my father while he muttered under his breath.

When I saw that my father was praying, I took his lead and began to pray silently for our trial to pass. My soul seemed to tell me that our trial was only beginning. I looked at my sister and wished that I could be as ignorant as she was. She began to talk to her doll about tea parties and travel to new lands. She told the doll that her dreams might come true to travel and see Paris. "*D* stands for Paris, you know," she told her doll.

Within twenty minutes a rickety train car with a horrid smell, worse than the camp, pulled into the train station. As soon as it stopped, guards opened the doors and placed a box up to the doors. Instead of helping ladies and girls in with a gentleness that I was taught to do, they would grab an arm and wrestle the person's weight into the car, normally hurling the person as a doll to the floor crumpled in a heap. As more people were piled into each car and past the point at which I might have thought who could comfortably have fitted into the car, each belonging was pitched in. We were nearly the last ones to be pitched in which produced a yelp from my sister yipping about the manhandling of her left arm. Once we were on the car, the doors whooshed shut. We heard a lever being lowered and a lock put in place. I looked back and forth from the people sandwiched in to the splintered wood frame of the box car. It felt as if I would be carved up by the splinters if I was pressed against it. Since I was closest to the door with others cramped in the center of the car, I was pushed along the door frame trying carefully not to have my face buried into the splinters. The jerking motion began with the first splinter lodging itself in my left cheek.

CHAPTER 10

Since our truck ride earlier that morning, I had thought that my body might be used to a jolting motion. After removing three splinters with my fingernails from my cheek, the motion of the car kept a steady rhythm with a rocking under my feet; the occupants took stock of their surroundings and circumstance. There was a feeling of despair and anxiety which pervaded more than the smell of rainfall we had noticed in the truck earlier that morning.

"Be anxious for nothing, but with prayer and supplication let your requests be known to God," my father's gentle voice reminded us.

I thought that I was making my requests known, but God wasn't listening. I wanted safety for my family who were being wronged; I should be in this place alone. After a few minutes, I firmly planted my cheek against the rickety wood. To my amazement, a miracle did occur. The boards around my face were not bleeding with more splinters but were worn smooth in my new spot. I wondered, as the rocking of the ride helped me forget where I was and where we might be going, who else might have placed his face against this board? Could mayors or pastors have been on this train? Could Frenchmen, Russian, German, or even Americans have placed their cheeks for the moments of solace against this smooth board as a beaten cutting board?

"How many other people have been on this train?" a voice in front of me exclaimed softly from a man with a black bruise rising on his left cheek bone and his right cheek against another smooth board such as mine.

"Don't know, sir," I said.

"You know, it doesn't even matter where they came from. We have all lost our citizenship. We all are less than cattle. I used to raise cattle north of here and placed many a cow on this type of car to go to the big cities after I had sold them. I could even now be riding on one of those cars I used to put..." the man with a black bruise upon his forehead rambled as he slid his fingernails against the smooth wood feeling for imperfections.

"You raised cattle?" I asked to be taken away from the reality we were living in.

"I thought that being a good German was all I had to do as well as feeding the German soldiers with my ranch. All of it meant nothing since I had an unwanted heritage. Nothing protected me from the Nazis. Now, I am going to Dachau." This last word seemed to bring many from their stupors with questions: *Why Dachau? How do you know? What will that mean to us? Will we find our families there?*

"Maybe we can find work there, and it won't be that bad. We can raise our families in peace without the Nazis hurting us anymore." A lady with her two-year-old child blurted out trying to convince herself more than anyone around her. Even I knew that Dachau would have no *good* work. I had never heard of the place they were talking about as a destination of doom, but I somehow felt it couldn't be good. Sure, I had heard of the town of Dachau, but all I could think about was the camp in the woods I had seen in the last year.

After more hours than I could remember had passed, we pulled to a stop in a place that had a smell that we could have sensed twenty minutes earlier. I thought it might be a feed lot that Mr. Black Bruise had visited when he was a rancher. The odor seemed much worse than anything I had smelled before. When the train jerked us to a halt, we could almost sense the putrid on our clothing; it vectored in all directions. After a few minutes more, the doors were flung open a few minutes more with shouts of "Get out now!"

We complied as quickly as we could not wanting to be pulled out and thrown to the ground. Unfortunately, many were flung down with sickening thuds and torn shoulders. I hurried down the one step and to the ground with my violin in my right hand and my suitcase in my left hand.

"Men to the right; women and small children to the left. All luggage must be left here. You will be given your luggage after we have checked it over for diseases. Put all luggage in the middle. Men to the right; women and small children to the left..." repeated in the bullhorn by several officers shouting in all directions at the same time. I started to put both my violin case and my suitcase in the middle, but Father told me to hang on to my violin and moved me along to the right.

As we parted into our lines, father and mother kissed briefly with mother pulling my sister away with her, and father taking me by the hand with him. I watched every step they took moving to the left until we were formed into a large semi-circle. It was almost amazing since there were innumerable semi-circles as far as the eye could see in both directions with an officer pulling a brown, wooden box to stand on.

As our officer stepped upon the box, a bedraggled man with grey and white striped pants, like those who come from an insane asylum, stepped up beside him with his head down. I looked up at father to see recognition of the prisoner in front of us dawning on his face. The prisoner then looked up around the circle and locked his eyes upon my father. I then saw who caused my father's jaw to slacken: Mr. Reinholdt. He was not the same man I had seen around our town. His cheeks were sunken in, and his waist could not hold his pants up without a rope around it. His beard didn't grow evenly between patches of white upon his face. He only nodded to us with a small smile as the officer began his recitations.

"You are entering the work camp of Dachau. I do not care how you came to us, or what your crime was. I do not care about your position before your criminal activities brought you to Dachau, but I care about the work we do here. Work well and you will live and eat. Work badly and you will join this one..." the officer pulled his pistol from his holster with practiced ease and quickly shot Mr. Reinholdt in the skull.

His body crumpled immediately from the knees first and then the torso with brains splattering almost everyone around him. Mothers had no time to shield their small children from this horror. The same horror was being played out as if a machine gun were being fired in rapid succession except the fact that each officer had one pistol and each semi-circle saw the same view I did. Cries shortly began from my mother's line, with children's whimpering following shortly thereafter. The officer motioned that a guard should take Mr. Reinholdt away as the officer walked quickly carrying his blood splattered box back to the camp gates. Tears fell from my father's eyes as they did from mine, not considering that this man had taken my first love away from me in Miss Paget, but that he was wasted with such brutality. I then felt a kinship with a dead man, because of the fate that I sensed we would share.

One of those little inane comments entered my brain and stayed for my duration in captivity; I no longer looked at these shiny booted officers as Nazis but rather demons and mentally referred to them as such. Nothing they did seemed to matter when considering our treatment. As we moved farther toward our *Demon's* destination, we moved farther away from my mother and Katrina. I didn't panic then but my father had a look of horror in his eyes, craning for another view of my mother.

"They are probably going to the women's camp a few gates over," he stated unconvincingly.

"When can we see them?"

"Don't know..." he trailed off straining for another look.

We began to be grouped into older and younger men, as well as boys who were very young. Those younger or the very old were pushed again to the left of us and were marched to another barrack with *Demon* disgust in their voices, seemingly angry over an "error in transportation." The *Demons* then asked if we had skills to perform within Dachau, for the "Glorious German Reich". When I had heard that even less than six months ago, my heart would swell with pride at being a patriotic German. At the time of entering the camp, when it was used by the *Demons,* I felt the curse of the words. We were pushed into lines to go to barracks depending upon the labor needs they considered useful. Only later would I find out that truly useful labor like my father's skill kept one alive a little longer. If you had no construction or necessary skill, the rock quarry became your destination. Father spoke up that he was a carpenter, and his son was a carpenter as well. As we were being moved to the "carpenter's line", one *Demon* started to take my violin away from me.

"Sir! He is a musician much like the ones in front of the gates. He is classically trained and can play any piece to soothe the most tired soul!" my father begged in statements that baffled me since none of it seemed to be true, even though because of the drama, I never heard them.

"Play something, scum!"

"Go ahead...your *Roses* piece."

Confused, I complied and pulled my bow out with the violin. As I played, shakily at first, our camp quarter seemed to quiet and slow. Years later many would say this as they threw footballs or baseballs in professional sports, even some musicians reported this feeling. The fascinating concept was that I noted that time slowed appreciably. The *Demons* moved slightly slower and more gently prodded their captives. People looked my way as they marched to their *Demon* determined destinations. I even calmed as I played, seeing the dancing brown and green trees in Ulm during a fall day six months earlier when I calmed Vonn with my bow. A tear started to fall with the memory of Vonn, and what must be happening to him and his family. As my shaking began again, the closest *Demon* stated, "Report to barracks 33A, musician's quarters!"

"But father is a pianist as well! He can play wonderfully!" I exclaimed.

"Moron, do you see any pianos here? He will stay with the carpenters," the *Demon* spit on the ground which landed upon my dusty shoes and turned away.

My father put his hand on my head, "It will be fine, you will see. Remember: *Your Word is life to those that find them and health to all their flesh.* I will see you in a little while. Go."

We were then lined up to a building called *Processing.* The only solace was that I had a few precious minutes to stand with my father hands clasped together. We listened with growing panic attacking my stomach to muffled screams within the *Processing* building. Our turn arrived too quickly since all I wanted was my father's hand and that line to never end.

The first *Demon* told us to strip out of our garments. Even if I completed this in record time, it didn't seem fast enough to the *Demon*. That *Demon* directed us by a shove to the hair cutting station, although it reminded me more of sheep shearing than the Ulm barber used to complete upon my head. With my violin case covering my privates, I received several scrapes (as well as my share of yelps due to the brutal shaving) from a striped man until my hands tingled from the pain upon my head.

I was then pushed forward toward a table in which they wrote on everyone's right arm. My right arm pinned to a bloody, wooden desk by an iron grip of a *Demon,* while another tattooed on my arm until I smelled my own flesh burn; the letters written in bloody ink upon my right forearm were *113589.* I had no idea what it meant, but my father received a number similar to mine only seconds after my branding. I was sure that my life was changed to being considered livestock from the cattle cars, to the sheering, and then finally to my branding without regard to my name. I didn't know why I couldn't be known by my name instead. With my right arm and my scalp dripping blood, I was pushed outside.

A man wearing striped clothing took me by my left arm, carefully trying not to irritate my bleeding right arm, to lead me to the musician's barracks. "Your father will be cared for since he is a carpenter. He will live. Those who are not useful die soon like the old and the young. Didn't you see the musicians as you came in? We are cared for as well enough since it makes the work continue in the quarries. Let me get you a place to sleep," the kind man hustled me away from my father.

One hour later, I lie in my bunk with only my violin case in my arms, deloused and in striped clothing like the rest of them, as well as the bloody cuts on my head that only trickled now. The torrent of emotions ran deep as the questions came to my mind.

"Where are my mother and Katrina? What work will they do? She is only five and can't do much yet. They can't be too rough with her. She will be frightened during the day without father. I could keep her with me as I play. Father could look on after her as mother sewed," I looked about seeking confirmations of my logic. As I searched the faces around me, my mind whirred with the reason of life for my family. They were "useful" as the kind musician told me.

They were, I willed.

No one answered me as they sipped their soup from rusty grey cans. My new musician friend brought me a black and less rusty can with steaming liquid that smelled like rotting vegetables pushing it to my mouth to drink. Against my better judgment, I did as I was told even though the taste and the smell scalded all of my senses.

"My name is Claus, I play the viola. I heard your tune. It was original, yes?"

"Yes, sir. I wrote it with father at the church in Ulm. He helped me write a few tunes that are unfinished to a great extent. I don't even have my music; it was in the suitcase I brought."

"We will help you remember it. As we play, we can help you reconstruct your music. There are many times to write as we play. It is difficult and takes an ability to play improvisationally, but you will catch on," Claus encouraged.

"Where are the women's barracks with my mother and Katrina? How can I find them? How can I find the carpenter's barracks where my father is?" I begged Claus.

"Your father will be fine. I told you that. He will live and get more rations than those going into the quarry."

"Why would they send my mother and Katrina to the quarries? They can't break rock?"

"Rest now, we have to rise early tomorrow before the others wake up."

"But..."

"Mind me, young man," Claus, with a stubbly chin and deep, brown eyes bore down on me.

"Yes, sir," I lay back slightly fearful of his tone. I had heard so much yelling for the last few days that I could not bear another scream. Rubbing my head carefully to dull my pain, I thought about those around the Musician's barracks. I later found out that Claus would never scream at me and would take a deep interest in my survival. Claus's face was sunken in showing off high cheekbones like almost every other inmate. His striped clothes hung off of him from a piece of a rope tied around his waist keeping his trousers up. I then appeared like everyone else except for the sunken cheeks. Within a few minutes, nothing mattered since I fell asleep from sheer exhaustion.

CHAPTER 11

The next morning I was awoken by Timothy and Claus, the head musicians of the camp. There was a loud clanging occurring before the sunrise much like a spoon hitting a can, only louder. We hurried out of our bunks to form lines. *Line forming* was a daily occurrence for all inmates, but ours occurred before the rest of the camp awoke. We had to set up so that the camp could hear our music. I found out later how large the encampment was and only a few sections had any music to wake up to, but the camp commandant had to be wrested awake by Richard Wagner. We would play outside of his quarters softly until he stepped outside of his doors, while the bloody ink from my right arm started to drip again upon my violin as it had all that morning.

Every morning was the same. Lines to count us were our clocks and a slight amount of rock-like bread that one was given which forced us to gnaw off the edges. Later, we would setup at a natural overhang as the rock quarry worked. Music was there to *calm the soul*, but I couldn't bear to watch the rock workers. If you stared long enough at the people, you could almost smell the death racking up like a score to a game that inevitably was set for these people to lose.

They stumbled and tripped over jagged, white rocks while carrying more rocks from one place to the other. I never realized what they were building, all they seemed to construct was death. The Germans would say, even in our earshot, that making Jews and Undesirables work with their hands breaking rock fittingly put us in our places since we were less than mules. They believed that we were fulfilling the calling of our lives in our deaths.

When a worker would trip and stay down, a *Demon* would begin a kind of beating I had never seen a dog take. If the person could not move anymore, he was shot on the spot. Sometimes, if he was a new worker, he was taken away to a infirmary of sorts. It really wasn't a hospital, because it lacked medicines and any health attributes. Rest might allow someone to recover enough to work another week more; the others died on their cots.

We continued to play from morning until after the workers paraded in roll call before soup was given. During the longest concert in my young history, I would roll my fingers on different edges to not develop a blister on one particular spot. If consistent discordance arose, the offending band member could be sent to the rock quarry. I saw two sent within the first three weeks of my arrival for three disharmonies, who were then kicked out of the orchestra. Most ensembles were a joy to play for since it wasn't work but pleasure that coursed through a musician's veins.

We played for our lives and for the backs of the audience. We felt that we were responsible for the morale of the workers. In the quarry overhang, we were allowed to play any composers we wished since mostly the *Demons* weren't listening to the music as much as the non-discordance of the music. We would change the tunes slightly but significantly enough in ways so that Jewish songs lifted up our brothers below. Even though I wasn't Jewish, we all considered ourselves kin since all were sent to die in some way or another. We always believed that they *recognized* the songs we played even if they were altered. Every day I looked for my mother and Katrina in the quarry as well as any paths I traversed. I kept a string vigil for them, praying and playing for their safety.

I realized that we were no longer operating by Ulm's civil rules when I met the *Captain Demon* of our section of the camp. He had long arms and legs which stretched him to more than six foot, four inches. When he grabbed one of us, the person felt the strength equal to three men within his grip. I really didn't meet him per se but was clutched by him. He would swat all of the newcomers as lines called *Ranks* were formed. He would hit each with enough force to knock most out of their stance, and then chide the poor soul for losing his balance. He popped me in the jaw enough that I bit my tongue hard and yelped in pain. His look told me to shut my blood soaked mouth.

"I am your Captain. I am to be addressed as 'Sir' at all times. Those of you who fail to play well will work the quarry. Instead of living in luxury on that ledge, you will break rocks for the Fatherland. All will be for a glorious death to serve the Fuhrer," the *Captain Demon* turned on his black and kicked the white powdery dust but not before expertly cracking his baton from his shoulder on the knee of the deprived soul standing at the end of the line. The man fell to his knees in pain.

When our *Captain Demon* would entertain other *Demons* or dignitaries, we were transferred from the natural overhang indoors. We were cleaned up so that we didn't "stink up the place" to play for his guests. I thought that it wasn't possible to hate a composer I had never met, but I loathed Wagner with a passion. Richard Wagner stood for all that was wrong with the *Demons* I saw daily as well as our *Captain.* I never was able to explain it more than that, but we still played our fingers off since doing otherwise meant the rock quarry. While in our hell, there was no variance allowed; no improvisation available to us. Only straight patriotic songs from Wagner or others written for the Fuhrer were allowed. We needed to sound like a crystal clear phonograph of the original piece. Fascinatingly, they never seemed to practice their music since these were amazing musicians. I, on the other hand, watched Timothy, who also played the violin, for the interludes. When I didn't know the piece well, I faked it until I learned it by heart.

What astonished me as the weeks passed in the *Demon* halls was how the war didn't seem to affect their sense of chivalry toward real women as the *Demons* called them. They would politely ask a woman to dance and gently take her by the hand to the pale wooden floor. They would laugh and twirl about as if they weren't in the middle of our hell. Many times I contemplated whispered yells of dignity, because I lost two inches to my waist in the first several weeks. Others were faring far worse than I was, including my father.

At times, I saw my father when he worked around the camp repairing buildings or pipes for the *Demons*. It seemed that the *Captain* took special pleasure at humiliating my father which made him slump his shoulders when he didn't notice me near him. I could see the beginnings of his cheeks sinking in and just as the sentence pronounced on the prisoners at the rock quarry. I prayed that the important work he was accomplishing would keep him alive, and that the *Captain* would quit beating him. The term *important work* meant so much more in the camp, denoting that one could receive a little more to eat and possibly live longer. I had no idea how much more, but that little amount that Timothy told me that we ate seemed still far too little for a boy like me in his teen years.

"Tomorrow I hope to bring you another piece of bread. Please eat it slowly when I give it to you so that it will last all night long," I saw my father through the craggy window sweeping pebbles away from a work area looking down as he labored.

"Father, I haven't been able to talk to you. You look pale...Has the *Captain* beat you?" I leaned out my broken window. To have a clear conversation with my father, I carefully stepped out into the warm night.

"Don't worry about me. I remember when I was a boy that I sometimes went for hunting trips with little to eat and lots of exercise with your grandfather. I'll be fine," he ignored my question about beatings I continued to see daily.

"Where are mother and Katrina? No one knows or will tell me. Are they in another barrack?"

A sadness filled his eyes instantly that he tried to hold back but could not. Tears came to his eyes faster than he wiped them away. "They were sent to their deaths. I checked the day after...after we arrived here. They are with the Lord now, son..." he trailed away as I fell into his left shoulder silently wailing. Before the camp, I would have wailed loudly, but here no one drew attention to himself. Father held me until our tears melted each other's shoulders.

"You must be brave and remember the Lord's words, 'Blessed are those who mourn, for they shall be comforted.' We have each other right now and as long as you are around, I draw strength from the Lord and trust in Him for your safety. Keep playing well and you will fulfill your dream....go son, I will see you tomorrow," Father shooed me away since the *Captain* would not allow prisoners to linger. His wrath would be fierce upon the backs of those caught in idle chatter.

I walked to my barracks hardly seeing the path through my tears. I hoped that Father was wrong about Katrina and Mother being gone, but I knew that he wasn't. The pain on his face indicated the embers of my vigil. I stumbled through the door of the barracks and forgot to shut the door behind me. Claus and Timothy saw me within 10 seconds of entering the Musician's barracks and read the grief in my face. Both flanked me with arms on my shoulders knowing that a death stare swam inside my eyes. I fell into Claus first then to Timothy as they embraced my face with me giving their chest baths they desperately needed.

Who is it? Timothy mouthed to Claus.

His mother and sister, I suspect. Claus' mouth replied.

I didn't remember anything more about that night and woke to a rainy day the next morning with bugles and screams. I rose slowly and held onto my head because my dead heart was pounding within my head. No more would I be comforted by my mother's sweet voice. I even longed to play with Katrina's dolls one more time and hear her incessant chatter about the doll's daily activities.

Standing upon the overhang, I played with my eyes closed most of that day. I waved my shoulders to the rhythms of the music allowing only the music to exist within my brain. I wanted nothing more from the world other than my father's existence. I would give my hands for his precious life and that became a continuous prayer for the next several weeks overlooking the rock breaking and dying backs of the workers.

As I played, watched and prayed in the next week, my mind hit upon a Scripture in Proverbs 24:11: "If thou forbear to deliver them that are drawn unto death, and those that are ready to be slain." My father would repeat that scripture during times when others were being led away by the Nazis to camps such as these. He questioned who would hold them back. I realized in that instant that my father had been the one who tried to do so.

The people whose knees were bending had no one to hold them back; no one to rescue them. My grief filled me deeper still until Claus responded to my heart's cry.

"Who will hold them back?" I stated as if to no one.

"We are..." Claus said back to me in a whisper only I could hear.

"How?"

"When we play, do you see how many look to our ledge?"

"Yes, but what does it matter?"

"It matters to them, Ernst. The solace that our music gives their minds allows another hour to pass. Our music shows them that loveliness still exists in the world," Claus explained the most beautiful truth I had heard in months, maybe years.

Our compositions held a magic, a treasure to all who heard it. It provided hope but I could not understand why. Claus did have the knowledge of that truth though, and I accepted his certainty. I prayed for that reality to blossom inside of all who heard our music. This in turn gave me hope. It seemed crazy to think of hope within a Scripture that really indicted those who did not help the innocent as again in Psalms 24:12 stated, "If thou sayest, Behold, we knew it not; doth not he that pondereth the heart consider it? And he that keepth thy soul, doth not he know it? And shall not he render to every man according to his works?"

I never knew verse 12 until Claus told it to me. He told me that the verse will be something that God will use to indict those Germans and the *Demon Captain*. The pain would be reconciled in the next life maybe even this one. Claus seemed to use this verse with an anger as he spoke it. It motivated him to hate, as he would put it. It gave me the opposite emotion, and I never knew why until later in my life. After the war when the German people would say that they never knew the camps existed hundreds of yards from their houses rang as hollow as a slackened bow across my strings. The truth of God's Word gave me hope that He knew there would be an end. That end was my goal: to see that end with my father intact as well.

A Violin's Secret

CHAPTER 12

As the months rolled into the first year, the calluses upon my left hand grew as well as my skill. While the work in the quarry progressed with a steady stream of new "volunteers", as the *Demons* would call them, my father somehow survived. But his existence, while he was far outliving the quarry workers, did not come without a cost. He lost two fingers within a pipe that he repaired for the *Captain* in one of the bathrooms. One pipe seemed to swallow his pinky and ring finger on his left hand. With no way of removing it without grease to do so, the *Captain* decided father didn't need the fingers anymore compared with the *precious* grease. Within one day, my father was back at work repairing anything that was needed within our dilapidation. He had more rations than the quarry workers, similar to mine, but his work was more arduous than mine. But without fail, he would sneak a speck of saw dust bread from his table into my hands.

One day when he delivered more saw dust to me, we heard a roaring in the distance coming closer every moment. I wondered if the heat of September 1944 was turning to a fall rain that would drench us until father pointed above to see swarms of bees in formation inking out the sky.

A Violin's Secret

"Our deliverance comes, son," father spoke in awe as he lifted a beaten red wrench he used upon most plumbing jobs within the camp.

"From bees?"

"No, from the Americans."

The Bees I thought I saw covered the clouds and began to drop nectar that was bitter to the Germans but sweet to our mouths. A few of the buildings he had repaired over the months were dying from the fiery nectar. I finally let go of my confusion to bask in the laughter of my father with his hope of deliverance. We laughed together for what seemed hours but were really only 10 minutes of bombing. We began to see these bombing runs as the only thing that would scare the *Demons*. We traded our sorrow for joy, while the *Demons'* creature comforts turned to pain.

The Bees returned daily. Not necessarily to bomb our camp or even in our area, but we saw them soar overhead nonetheless. Every time we saw them we cheered; although you could not cry outwardly since it would anger the *Demons* more than disobedience. We felt some level of hope, but I felt none for my father.

His shoulders dipped even more when he walked. When I asked him about it, he said it was because he had to lean over fixing sinks. I could see that he was hurting more and more. His face took on a yellowish tint while I tanned up making me appear healthy compared to him. Father also started to pull up his trousers more daily as he walked away from me. Claus and Timothy shared a knowing glance that I couldn't understand as my father would leave. When I tried to ask them what they might know about my father's condition, they would tell me that he looked fine to them -- but everyone knew better.

That next day, I tried to find my father, which was a chore since most minutes of the day were accounted for by the *Demons.* I began to look through the plumbing routes he would take from one set of pipes to another until I ran into the *Demon Captain.* He held out his hand to backhand me aside as a Bruno had done to me before. I crumpled to the mud which splashed on my cheeks and looked up at him in surprise.

"Where are you going, pig?" he spat his words at me.

"I am looking for my father, Captain Sir," I quickly rose to my feet and bowed my head in deference.

"Not today, get back to your barracks before I beat you," while he swung his stick upon my left shoulder to make me run away.

As I started to turn away, I saw my father not more than ten paces away taking a giant step toward me with obvious protection in his mind, but I beat a hasty retreat so the beating wasn't my father's that night. For many days or nights after that, whenever I tried to find my father, it felt as though the *Demon Captain* was there looking for me. Each time his hand forced me away with more blows, but I didn't care about them as much as the chance to see my father. Even those brief glimpses filled me with despair.

His body was decaying further daily until I turned a corner one day in search of my father again to find him huddled on the ground protecting his head from the *Captain's* baton. His blows alternately struck another body part on my father where his arms and hands were not protecting himself. I ran to them screaming for the *Captain* to stop.

"*Captain...Captain...*The *Commandant* is calling for you, sir!" I lied trying to get him to stop beating my father. The last blow was reserved for me as his face reddened in disgust as he backhanded the club and hit me on the chin. I dropped like a sack of flour spilling to the ground. Amazingly, father crawled to me a few seconds later to check on me! After the beating I had seen him take and the ones I had not seen, he still used what little energy he had to check on me. Tears welled up for his concern which he interpreted as pain for my blow.

"Did he hurt you badly, Ernst?" with a concerned bloodshot left eye looking down on me.

"No, father, I had to stop him!"

"Oh, *son...son...*please don't do that again!" he coughed out in a horse whisper. "I can handle what he might give me. 'God will never give you more than you can handle.'"

"But father, you are d...dying," I sobbed.

"That may be son, but you must remain strong. You must survive for my sake, if not for your own. I want you to live. Promise me you will not interfere and cause harm to come on you again."

"But he was *killing* you!"

"If God releases me from this body, I will go. I only wish I could...protect...y..." he trailed off with tears that I had rarely if ever seen him dredge up. It was not that he couldn't feel things deeply, but he didn't let his own tears be known by me.

I held my father gently for a long time there. It seemed as though time stopped. We were father and son sitting at a picnic in the grass. He stroked my greasy hair and comforted me as much as it seemed to clean my grimy face with his tears. It seemed that he was not concerned anymore about hiding his emotions from me. A terror rose within me thinking that he was giving up his life and saying his goodbyes, but his head caresses slackened my sorrow. I closed my eyes and thought of the meadow outside of our house that seemed thousands of miles away, almost dream-like in its fantasy. I longed for those easy days where I could go to school and Bruno might even throw a dirt clod on the back of my coat. I then thanked God for those memories of the meadows and asked Him to lock them into my heart forever.

When I sat up, both of our composure returned and a calm girded me. I told myself that he would live, and we would make it out of this hell together. We hugged goodbye and I sauntered to my barracks for the night.

That night I told Claus and Timothy all that had happened in the mud with my father. They listened to me prattle on that my father was going to be fine and he was going to make it. Even though I knew I didn't believe it and they didn't either. Not a soul in the barracks would contradict hope when it was spoken unless the man speaking it was obviously losing his sanity. It was easy to lose your faculties but hard to hold onto your hope. The men would ease my illusion with calming words and listening to hope with quiet and thoughtful nods to those who spoke it.

Our barrack musicians were called to more disgusting parties of the *Demons*. Instead of the demure looking social events in earlier times at the camp I witnessed, it was now pure debauchery: laughing, carousing and loud drunken bellowing songs that would even drown out our playing. They wanted up-beat type music which was so foreign to the moods of those with not enough to eat. We watched them dance and consume in front of us as if we weren't there, as if we couldn't smell the food. These parties continued for the next week, because we found out that there was a new camp Commandant coming. The old one left for unknown reasons and the new one wasn't here. Some of the higher-ups were missing as well; the *Demon Captain* was running these parties for the time being.

Nothing he touched or did seemed to be of redeeming value. As he would walk by the stage where we played, he tried to take a drink or eat something in front of us. If it was food, juices or frosting would leave stains upon his mouth and chin. I began my love affair with hatred for this beast. He was so much like Bruno until that thought hit me... the *Demon Captain* was Bruno's **father**. I had seen him a few times growing up in Ulm. When I passed him in this camp, I tried not to look deeply into his eyes because doing so would invite scrutiny no prisoner wanted. But in this party, catharsis came by realizing who he was and who his son was growing up to be like. That realization made me miss one of the first notes I had missed in many months. Luckily for me, no one on the dance floor noticed in their stupor, and

I paused for a second to gain my composure again to continue this gay music I loathed.

That next week when the camp Commandant arrived, the parties thankfully ended and our temptation was broken. When you have so little to eat, you sometimes can fake your body into believing the hunger pangs aren't what they really are. When someone eats something in front of you, your body responds too deeply to be fooled; then the hunger grows worse, and it was nearly debilitating.

With our normal schedule returning to the top of the overhang for our brothers and fathers, I tried to find my father near dark again. I found a more crumpled man than before being kicked by the *Demon Captain*. After the *Demon Captain* left the crumpled man, I ran to him only to find it was not my father.

"Do you know where my father is? He used to do the plumbing and the carpentry...is that what you are doing too?"

"Yes, boy..." he said with a wheeze. "I am the replacement. The other one died two days ago. I was promoted from the quarry. It was my lucky...lucky day," he spit up a small hunk of blood over his left shoulder with a wry smile.

I backed away from him in horror at his revelation. He said it with the casualness of a man who had seen more death than a boy should witness. As soon as I left his field of vision with his left eye swollen shut, he retreated into his own world and picked himself up along with his tools. He began to pound a lead pipe with that *beaten red wrench* my father had used. The crumpled man's pounding secured the knowledge of my father's death, and there I collapsed like the new plumber falling into his bed for the night.

No one seemed to notice my sorrow; no one comforted me even though several walked by from time to time. Grief was too big of a pit that would swallow anyone whole and make one unfit to work: one's own death sentence since work was the only thing that kept anyone alive. After what seemed hours, I picked myself up enough and plodded my way back with my failure to keep my father alive. I collapsed into Timothy's arms who again instantly knew the reason for my despair and held me throughout that night.

The next several days I went through the motions of playing. Many times my fellow musicians would cover for me musically since there were several silent periods from my violin. The only thing I did that was a blessing is to keep my bow posed over my violin giving the appearance of playing. I had lost my will to live, but Timothy and Claus would not allow me to give up. Even though I was all of 14 years old and a man in most people's eyes, I needed a father figure; I received two older brothers that ordered me around as the opposite of the *Demons*, with kindness and gentleness. They planned my days until a month had passed from my father's death. At that time I able to play again all the day long without breaks, but only then was I beginning to think about a new course of action: revenge. While I would never know who had killed my father, the consequences of many beatings or the lack of food, for all I knew or cared, the *Demon Captain* had completed his murder. And I would complete that *Bruno's father's* death if I could find a way.

The poisonous odor my spirit was pouring out, even though I was silent about my thoughts and intentions, must have alerted Timothy and Claus. They had sensed that I had made a decision to kill for my father's death by an equal death. After our pitiful supper of steamed broth, they quietly challenged me back in our barracks.

"I know, son, that you blame yourself for your father's death. But, you mustn't," Timothy pleaded with me.

I stared at him with confusion and then anger since I didn't blame myself for his death, at least I didn't believe so at that time.

"Timothy is right. You were not to blame and you shouldn't plan rash things against yourself, Ernst," Claus held my thin shoulder with his spindly right hand.

Again, I stared in at the both of them with the confusion winning the fight over anger by a giant margin. I had no idea what they were saying, but I realized that they knew I was making a plan.

"What are you saying?" I muttered.

"Don't try and harm yourself. Too many try to drown the pain inside their own death. We have seen it before and it leads to nowhere," Timothy pleaded again.

"It would lead to Heaven," I quietly countered. Finally understanding what they were saying considering this new option that I had not thought about before. For days after that, I contemplated how *I* could die. It was so ironic to find a way to die in a self-proclaimed death camp. For most people suffering in the quarries, if death was even slightly conceived of, it was relatively instantaneous. For me, it was only slightly harder. If I ate much less, it would be painful but just as sure. I could also walk toward a fence; run at a guard with a murderous look; slug the *Demon Captain*; or numerous other infractions which would lead toward death. My problem with death was two-fold: my father's ghostly voice in my ear dissuading me from suicide, and my fear of the physical pain of death. Even though I had endured plenty of pain, the latter concept grasped me firmly, shaking me from its course. After those gloomy days of contemplation in which I was placed on an infirmary bed by my friends, I snapped out of it. I am not even sure how I did it, but I believe that I grieved enough. All that was left was my father's quoting of Scripture that lead me on.

CHAPTER 13

While the winter dragged into 1945, I could see the hopelessness transfer from the prisoners to the *Demons*. The inmates' load seemed to lighten with every bombing raid they heard overhead. The Bee cacophony filled their hearts with hope from the West where the rumors of the Americans coming were whispered behind each flimsy bunk. While our dreams soared toward freedom, the quarry backs began to stoop deeper from the cold. 1945's beginning was especially frigid all over Germany. It was almost as though Hell was screaming its unholy wind calling the *Demons* home. And the *Demons* seemed to know it. Some of them stopped shaving; their clothing became tattered and unkempt. The work in the quarry ground to a halt during the daily *Duck and Cover* events all of us played with the boulder nearest to us. The rocks were even colder than usual.

One day, in late March, we were ordered to assemble outside of the Commandant's quarters. We were given a piece of *Saw Dust* and a cup of soup (we were reminded to take a blanket and draped them around our shoulders). We were counted by barracks and told to follow in two lines per barrack. We were then told that those of whom didn't keep up were to be disposed.

"Let's move out," was our only warning of our departure by the *Demon Captain*. And we walked out of the camp. The worst of us were left behind, while we were considered useful to work in other factories. I carried my blanket and my violin case, as did all of the other musicians. For the first several miles of our journey we saw no one on the roads. My violin slapped against my thigh on an off-rhythm beat to our marching.

As the march halted for the night, most of us had made it to a clearing. A few did not. Gunshots heard behind me were the only reminders of death. I sat next to Claus and Timothy as we huddled for warmth against Hell's 1945 Wind. We were so tired that the guards really didn't have to remind us not to escape. I could have made the hike many times in my youth (my *youth* was considered the time before Dachau). The food and conditions didn't allow me to retain my breath that night since only shivers kept me gasping. No one talked since that took too much energy. We tried to eat our *saw dust* and sleep as much as possible for our next day's journey.

The next two days followed the same pattern of walking and no talking while shots fired to the rear in growing numbers. Sleep was harder to come by, because our stomachs awoken us when our bodies relaxed enough to sleep. The morning of the third day, we waited for the order to march again but it never came. The musicians were probably in the best shape and had found that we were maybe a few hundred feet ahead of the group that left Dachau. The *Demons* who had led us had deserted us in the night. Confusion and then panic danced in my brain. Sedated elation erupted from the older musicians understanding what I could not: we were free, for the time being.

We musicians began to walk off of the road with Claus leading the way saying that he knew a route to get us to a town closer from where we had heard the Americans were coming. We walked with purpose (or as much as starving souls could) through a road from our captivity to our freedom. Each step farther away brought about renewed hope. I occupied my time with inane details: a flock of birds through a clearing that landed upon two burned trees as they gathered for a church service. There was a continual attention to a voice in the wind that only the birds could hear. I longed to join their church and consider the comforting words from a Bird Pastor's kind heart; words I hadn't heard in almost two years within our Hell.

Further on through our *road of hope* I saw some undamaged trees that danced in the wind rhythmically to a beat that only the wind sang. I began to sway with the same rhythm that the trees heard until my violin rudely bumped into Timothy. He steadied me as if I were about to fall. Timothy then asked for Claus to stop so that we might forage for some food along the spring grounds. Several berries along three bushes clumped together, of which Clause told us were non-poisonous. Each gobbled them until lips were stained as if we had chewed on a wild beast's bloody innards. I then realized that the picture I saw in each of the four remaining men with us of reddened mouths and some level of bodily satisfaction with our meal seemed to be much how the *Demon's* looked as they beat us which gave them great joy.

For two more days, we wound our way through the brush and evergreens until we stopped in a clearing. As we reached it, I sensed we knew this place through my personal haze. I believed for a time that I was dreaming since I had not traveled much at all through my homeland, but the groans of the men with me confirmed my reality that we had wandered back to the camp. Something was different though since I heard no sounds of rock breaking within the quarry.

We then saw the sign that I thought meant that there were Christians close, a reddened cross. I ran to one and asked him to pray for me, that I needed God to lead us home. A confused man in a green burlap coat scrunched his face in confusion, but realized I needed food and water. He led me to the bumper of another cross colored in red on a truck in which he produced a bowl of hot soup and bread. Every time that I tried to gulp the soup in one swallow, he pulled my hand down telling me in broken German to slow down. His gentle resistance against my gut repeated a dozen times until I finished the food. When I finished it, I collapsed in relief. The man who wore the cross in red took me in his arms and carried me to the *Demon's* Barracks. I tried to squirm out of his strong grasp looking backward to see my violin with what little strength I had left in fear of a beating. He was unbowed from his commitment to lay me on a *Demon's* cot. I weakly asked where he had placed my violin. He covered me, and ordered me gently to sleep. I complied for more than two days.

During those two days of sleep when I rolled fitfully, I heard gunshots that didn't really stir me enough from my sleep since I had heard those for the past two years constantly through the days and nights. I awoke to Timothy sitting by my bed bringing me more soup which tasted more wonderful than I thought that food could ever be. He pulled the cup from my lips eight times to slow my ravenous progress. Later, I arose from my bed only slightly unsteadily to a slowly milling congregation of people. The first groups were the green group I had met when we walked back into camp.

"That's the Americans, Ernst," Timothy answered my unspoken question. "They have paraded through here with high level officers, since we arrived from our walk. They lined up some of the guards and camp officers at first to shoot them for their crimes, until the higher ranks arrived to stop this. I can tell you that I have never felt much of a lust for vengeance..." he trailed off not completing the thought.

We walked out of the barracks to see a disgusted gaggle of other people who stared all around them and held their noses; the ones closest to us looked upon us with horror. I even recoiled from their revulsion.

"Why are they doing that?" I asked quietly of Timothy.

"We smell and look bad. I heard that some of their generals gathered the towns around Dachau to make them help in the burial of the dead." To my left, I saw townsfolk much like the ones I saw back in Ulm carrying the bodies to massive grave pits with scarves around their noses and mouths.

Timothy and I walked slowly about the camp inspecting our old prison. Once a man with a large camera, bigger than I had ever seen, asked in English if he could take our picture. Timothy said that it would be OK to do so and he put his arm around me for the photograph. Neither of us could smile since we hadn't smiled since we arrived. The reporter asked if I was Timothy's son or younger brother.

Timothy exclaimed something in English to the reporter and moved on. Along the northern fence line close to the guard towers, I saw a line of dead bodies in grotesque angles in their death throes in front of the barbed fence.

"Who are they?" I asked as we passed by no more than twelve feet away from the fence.

"Those are the guards who were killed in the first hours after we were liberated. We killed a few as well as some of the Americans."

One of the *Demons* had a high ridged cap falling from his head. I recognized the uniform and it drew me closer until I saw through the blood-stained face this torturer: *the Demon Captain.* In his left hand he held a picture of his son and his wife: Bruno when he was only six or seven years old. I stared at the picture for several minutes trying to see myself back before this horror that had wrought upon me. I turned my head to the side mentally stammering for the images of my youth that would not seem to come. I had known someone named Bruno, but I could not recall anything except the distain that he showed for me near the end of my time in Ulm.

As I thought of Ulm and the disdainful look, the flood of memories hit me of my mother, Katrina, Miss Paget, and father. I bowed my head quickly and wailed tears that washed the dried blood from the photograph. Timothy rushed to my side to console me. As he lifted me up from my grief under my armpits, I plucked the photo from the dead man's grasp and bent it into a "U" shape in my palm. The tears would not stop flowing even though I had finally controlled my wail.

Anger began to burn within me as I saw these people lifting the bodies of their own countrymen that they helped to murder by their silence. As we moved through them toward Timothy's destination inside of his arms around my shoulders, the people parted and looked away in disgrace. I stared each of them down and kicked dirt clods in their direction as we passed as my own indictment of their torture of patriotic Germans who they had helped to kill, hoping that my dust would kill.

Timothy took me to a small barrack that had that cross symbol on it. We passed under the door hang and Timothy looked for a cot for me to lie on. I sat on it for minutes or hours staring at the site outside of bodies being moved until I noticed a girl beside me waving her hand before my face.

"Do you understand German?" she said.

"Of course, I do," I stated incredulously.

"Well, I called for you three times and you didn't seem to hear me."

"I am sorry, this all makes so little sense," I gestured with my nose toward the door with all the townsfolk.

"Actually, it is the one thing that does make sense. Requiring the people clean up what they started is the only way I am going to get any level of vengeance. I am too weak to do more, unlike your friends over there," she motioned toward Timothy and Claus over my right shoulder. Claus looked different and had blood splattered on his collars. He didn't appear to be injured.

"Did Claus do something?"

"You might put it that way. Being one of the few that had any muscle among us, he led a charge at the guards after the Americans arrived. With the Americans help, they killed most of the men against the northern fence," She stated matter-of-factly, exactly where the *Demon Captain* had died with his picture of his son that was still bent in my hands. "What is your name?"

"Ernst...and yours?"

"Ileana. I loved your playing in the orchestra," she replied.

"Thank you, and where did you work?"

"I was the Captain's maid," she gestured over her left shoulder toward the fence line that I had been to.

"It must have been horrible to be around the *Demon Captain*," I quipped.

"That is an interesting name for him. I wish I had thought of it before. His beatings would have made more poetic sense..." I puzzled at her statement since no beating ever made sense to me.

I stared at her for a few minutes, a girl by whom I was captivated. She had a full head of brunette colored hair (which was unusual to see among us) and spindly fingers in which I imaged the piano keys would fit nicely. Her blue eyes were stark against her pasty white face smeared with layers of dirt. Of course like the rest of us, she was as gaunt as anyone could be and still be alive. She must have been not too much older than me; I guessed 16 or 17 years old. She had told me that her father had died fighting in Poland in 1939 in the first days of the war. Her mother and she were deemed dispensable due to a rechecking of their Jewish heritage.

After we gobbled more of the soup that Timothy had given the both of us, Ileana and I never separated from one another. We decided to find her mother's necklace and my violin. Each morning for the next week, we would walk the perimeter and then through the rows of bodies; the walk became our exercise mentally and physically. Every pile we found, we would sort through looking for the last items to our past. So many piles of stolen articles were amazing to the Americans (I had learned a little English through my weeks in the camp as well as realizing I had a talent for languages I never knew before). Piles of glasses, shoes, pants and pictures were all over the camp, overturned from the stacks of items from the *Demon's* barracks. It meant nothing for a *Demon* to suddenly be wearing an article that had great significance to those inmates around him, knowing that there was nothing left of their loved ones other than the ashes that rained throughout most days we lived in the camp.

We looked inside of another barrack marked *VERBOTEN.* In the past, I would have never considered even peering at the door, much less trespass upon the sign. As we opened the door, more neat and orderly piles of items of more value were categorized on shelves. Three shelves into our search, we found Ileana's brooch.

"Thank you for returning to me what was once stolen," she cried.

"Were you praying just then?"

"I don't know why I said that...no, I wasn't praying. My family didn't follow the decrees of my grandparents. We integrated ourselves into Poland until it no longer desired us. Now I have no God and no Land, only you," she said with only a slight sadness to her voice.

"My God is all I have left, except you, that is," I replied not trying to preach.

"Let us go look for your violin," she changed the subject and our environment by pulling me out of *VERBOTEN.*

Later that afternoon, we stumbled upon my violin still in its case but the hinges were slightly ajar. I tried to close it, but they were bent. I carefully angled them back with Ileana's help. I beheld my cherished violin with an almost instant rage when I saw a large scratch running its length. Someone had bruised my father's handiwork with almost as much brutality as I had been treated. Sensing my reddened face, Ileana touched my face to begin to calm the storm in me.

"This can be repaired. But, on the other hand, instruments with scratches can be your reminder of where we have been and our survival. Their history is our own."

Instantly, I realized that she was right. All around me upon the ground, I saw other instruments mostly broken or damaged beyond recognition, let alone repair. My violin had suffered through the Time and survived, as I did as well. Ileana gently brushed the dirt from the case and latched it shut. She picked the instrument up and reached for my hand as well.

A Violin's Secret

CHAPTER 14

The Present

"**P**apa, that's how you met Nana!" Axel exclaimed.

"Yes, little buddy. We got married a few months later and one year from when the Americans had liberated the camp, we came to America," Ernst had been walking and talking for so long that he had to swallow hard to remove some of the hoarseness from his voice. As he did so, he noticed that Rachel had paced only one step behind the arm-in-arm parade that Axel and Ernst made. Rachel had red and swollen eyes with her mascara mostly losing their shape.

"I'm sorry," Ernst spoke to Rachel for how he perceived the story affected Rachel. "Maybe you didn't really want to know about your grandparents...and aunt."

Rachel touched Ernst's shoulder with intensity in her stare, "Dad, I am *so glad* that you did. The pieces of the story never truly helped me put it all together until now. Now, I know about the Aunt Katrina and the grandparents who I wished I had known." Rachel leaned into to hug her father confirming for Ernst that he had made the right choice in telling the both of them the whole story.

"Dad, do you mind if I ask you a few questions?" Rachel cautiously asked.

"That's why we are having this walk," Ernst stated.

"What happened with Bruno and Werner? Did you ever find out who had turned you in?"

"I never found out who actually turned the family in. I wondered about it for a long time and hated both for their perceived role in our torture. I blamed myself for years in between the seething for Bruno and Werner for our family's final condition. I had heard it called something like *survivor's guilt* much like the kids at Columbine felt who made it out of the library. As we went to Ulm to find anyone left alive that I knew, I found out that none of the boys that I had known growing up had survived the war. The town was not bombed in a campaign like Dresden or Berlin.

"I did find out by talking to Werner's mother that Werner and Bruno were drafted several months after my family was taken away. Werner's mother received her son's medals by courier and a letter congratulating her on her heroism on losing her son. She told me that Werner died two days into the Battle of the Bulge, as we Americans put it. She also said that Bruno had died in Berlin fighting the Russians in the last days of the war.

"It took me years to stop hurting myself about my family. For years before you were born, I could hardly touch my violin without tears. As I moved on, I even forgave my violin, too," Ernst said with a smile and a wink which eased the depth of the discussion for Rachel as well.

"Did Nana die because of her wounds in battle?" Axel scrunched his face trying to rectify his Papa's past.

"No, she died ten years ago as most of us do when we get older. We had a great life together after the war."

Rachel knew that her father had many difficult days when she was younger battling his own depression, partially because of a new and struggling business as well as from his own reckoning of the past. Rachel had heard very little other than the basic facts that her father was a holocaust survivor, and that her extended family did not exist outside of her father and mother. She watched *Schindler's List* and *The Hiding Place* as well as a movie that had come out in DVD about Dietrich Bonhoeffer who was a pastor during World War II who had spoken out against the Nazis treatment of the Jews. All movies educated her to a segment of her father's unspoken past but only made her long for the words that he had for Axel and her during the walk around the lake.

"Dad, this was the most special gift you could have possibly given us. Thank you for sharing it with..." she could not finish the sentence and hugged her father again. Axel joined in the hug as children do who do not wish to be left out of an opportunity of expression.

"It is not really a gift, but I knew that Axel needed to know and now I realize that God brought you today to hear the story. Pass it on so that you may draw strength from it. I lost so much strength after the camp, but in the last few months and years, it has been a source of courage to face my cancer."

Rachel could only nod her head in acceptance of what he was really saying that Axel could not understand: Ernst had ordained that this was his last days upon the Earth. Nothing was going to stop him from entering eternity soon. He seemed peaceful about his choice even though her soul cried out for more hopeful medical options to extend his life. She knew he could never allow a slow deterioration of his mental and physical faculties.

"Dad, I don't even know how to ask you this...do you have a...a reason why you survived and others did not? I don't mean to be rude or suggest..."

"I know what you mean and anyone asks that question after trauma. After much prayer, I only have one answer: it is because of the violin..." Ernst trailed off.

"Do you have any pictures of Aunt Katrina and your parents...I mean my great-grandparents?" Axel asked.

With a long sigh and a longer face, Ernst replied, "I wish I did." He had thought of little more than a simple picture of all three of them in the last five years since he moved into Concordia. He had seen some of the war documentaries with these precious pictures that even the young had spirited away. He had cursed himself for years for not taking the effort to find pictures.

"When your mother and I tried to go to my old home after the war, the family who lived in my old home would not allow us inside. We pleaded through sobs that I only wanted the pictures of my parents and my sister killed in Dachau, but it had no effect. The man of the old home stated that everyone had lost family including two of his sons within the Luftwaffe. He had thrown out our *garbage* the year before in 1944. The man slowly shut the door on my face with Ileana's tears still wet on her face and my arm around her leading us toward town," Ernst reminisced.

"We walked through my old stomping grounds, but I had never felt more like an outside, even within the rotten camp. Dachau was more of a home to us at that time than the town that completely disowned me."

"We must leave Germany. This is not your home...maybe it never was," Ileana had said at the time.

Ernst realized many years later that his wife had never spoken truer words than those. Germany was not his home. It seemed to be a home of a boy within the movies more than the home of his youth. After their visas were approved, Ileana and Ernst departed for America.

"Were those letters you used to write to Uncle Timothy and Uncle Claus the same ones from the camp?" Rachel jogged her own memory of addressed letters her father would send to these two men.

"Yes, one-and-the-same. They moved to Israel and helped defeat the Arabs during 1947 and again in 1967. They sent me a picture of the two of them in an orchestra near Haifa, Israel. I will get those to you as well. Claus never married and the two were closer than blood brothers after they had lost their own families during our hell. There was a bitterness that I could never break through during my correspondence with them. There was always hatred for the Germans, British, and the Arabs which stayed the country in its infancy and still does to this day. They told me to call them 'Uncle' and that the name gave them comfort knowing that they saved one from a Dachau death.

"Claus died in 1989 of pneumonia when he was 65 years old. Timothy got married only after Claus died. Timothy died ten years later, only two years after your mother died."

The three walked on for many minutes in complete silence (rare for a youngster to do). Each was contemplating the information given and received, creating new sets of memories or dredging up the past. Ernst had long ago dealt with his guilt and anger. He knew that Claus and Timothy never did. He noticed that through his correspondence and even the occasional phone call, the anger killed the two "Uncles" daily. Ileana and Ernst both learned to put it behind them as Ileana accepted Yeshua in the 1970's. Both attended a Messianic Jewish congregation in south Denver for many years.

The sun began to splatter the sky with its orange and blue hues called a *Denver Bronco Sunset* as Ernst flipped his silver pocket watch open. They had walked, talked, stopped and ate a baloney sandwich that Axel had proudly made during that several hour monologue, and all seemed to lose energy. He knew there was some time allotted for questions in the next few weeks, but as they turned off the lake's walking path, Axel had another.

"Papa, does your tattoo still bleed?" Axel was always trying to put together the pieces of the past with his present realities.

Ernst didn't answer that question for a few moments to try to staunch a new flow of tears. He hadn't expected a question to pierce that deeply into his heart. They opened the door to his building then his apartment and stepped over to his violin before he had the ability to answer.

"Only when I think of father, mother and Katrina..." Ernst moved the violin to his chin. Rachel had heard the haunting melody in *A minor* before, but then heard it for the real first time as she silently wept while staring upon the scratch in his violin while Ernst played *Roses.*

A Violin's Secret

Author's Post Script:

There are doubtless many emotions when considering the Holocaust as a whole. I have personally studied everything to do with World War II since I was in grade school. The one lingering image that has haunted me is the rows of barracks packed into a small area within Dachau and Auschwitz, just to name a few. Only the stupid or deliberately diluted can wave the magic wand to dispel the reality of the Holocaust which took the lives of six million Jews and five million of other citizens in Europe.

Some who might have heard that only the Jews suffered did not meet the soldiers of the allied forces imprisoned in work camps. Several European countries chose to round up citizens for resistance fighting against the Nazi invaders, and anyone who hid Jews. The citizens of Germany were taught all through the 1920-1930's that the Jews were a rat-infested race of greedy sub-humans. Is it any wonder that when these individuals gave up their rights to think independently and they joined the Nazi party? Many who hadn't really thought the subject through believed the propaganda hook, line and sinker.

Sadly the answer is *no*. I had met a Teacher's Assistant in English who grew up in Germany; she always scared the me when I was in seventh grade in Parker Junior High in Colorado. When I came back in 1988 as a Student Teacher in that same school where I grew up, this same woman, who I came to love, told me amazing stories that awed me of how she got into the Hitler Youth. When this courageous woman learned of Hitler's true disposition and the atrocities of the Nazis, she tried several times to take her own life. One day at a teaching seminar, she recalled to me that she tried to open an aircraft to drift to her death. The fictional characters of Werner and Bruno were typical youths who were swayed by the fervor around them to commit acts of insanity thinking that the Nazis offered the sane solution.

There were also many countless brave men and women who chose to staunch the sick plague of Nazi ideals to kill off any perceived inferior race. They constantly resisted their fear for their families as well as their own fears of being caught in the act of treachery against the Fuhrer.

There are still circles of influence years after World War Two who sadly blame organizations and religions for what the Nazis gruesomely referred to as the Final Solution to rid Europe of Jews and other Undesirables. Was Germany a Christian nation and did Christians kill the Jews because the Jews killed Christ? This is an unfortunate blanket statement not born of fact. Anyone who commits murder does not have Christ in his or her heart. No, there is no Christian nation, not even America which was founded upon Judeo-Christian ideals. If a nation can enter the kingdom of Heaven, then the path to Heaven is not a narrow path as the New Testament states. Only those who, "confess his name and believe within his heart that Jesus is the Christ," really are believers. Nothing the Nazis did was Christian.

Actually, much evidence suggests that Hitler and the Nazi regime was conceived more out of the Occult than anything within the Bible. Hitler even stated that Christianity was an enemy of the state. And, certainly it was. Consider this book a perseverance of the human spirit with the guidance of the Holy Spirit within a ghastly time in the 20th century. I dedicate this story to those who lived through the Holocaust and to those who discovered it. Daily their minds are DVD memories to a time that very few will know first-hand.